Cowboy
Blue

Cat Johnson

ISBN-13:978-1540482136
ISBN-10:1540482138

PROLOGUE

Twenty years ago

Casey Harrington stood on tiptoe in her pink sneakers to reach the display above her head. She touched the box's front cellophane panel with one fingertip. "Isn't he beautiful?"

Her older sister, Jody, shook her head. "Boy dolls can't be beautiful, silly."

"Sure they can." Casey tried to hide her pout.

What did stupid Jody know anyway? The Cowboy Cody doll on the toy store shelf was beautiful to her, with his blue denim shirt that matched his eyes perfectly and his brown cowboy hat that sat atop his light brown hair.

She tried to peer past the cardboard to get a look at the cowboy boots popping out from the bottom of his jeans.

It was hard to see in the box, but she knew from having seen him on the television commercials so many times that his boots were a beautiful brown leather.

She wished she had a pair just like his, but if it was a choice between asking for Cowboy Cody or a pair of boots, she was definitely going to ask for Cody.

Casey wasn't taking any chances by putting two things on her Christmas list when there was only one thing she really and truly wanted. Only one gift she couldn't stand the thought of living without. Cowboy Cody.

Jody, a whole twelve-years old and acting like she was way more than just four years older than Casey, folded her arms. "Can we go look at some other stuff now?"

"No. I want him." Casey stood her ground.

Jody rolled her eyes dramatically. "I'm sure this toy is meant for boys, not girls. If you insist on getting a doll, why don't you ask Mom for the new Barbie? She comes with a really cool dress and matching luggage."

Casey shot her sister a look of disbelief. Who could possibly want another old Barbie when they could have Cody? "I don't want Barbie. I want him."

"Whatever. Come on. Let's go. Mom's probably looking for us by now."

"No. She said we could shop by ourselves for half an hour."

"And we've been here for like an hour already staring at that boy doll."

"Fine." Dragging her feet so heavily the rubber soles of her sneakers squeaked against the store's floor, Casey followed her sister.

She glanced over her shoulder at the object of her desire one last time before they turned the corner.

Just looking at him made her heart flutter.

Cody and his cowboy code—that was the focus of each weekly episode of the Cowboy Cody Show that had her glued to the TV every Saturday morning.

It made Casey wish she lived on a ranch out west like Cody's, instead of in stupid Connecticut.

There were no horses, no cowboys, no prairies, nothing fun where she lived. Just rows of houses that all looked the same with little tiny patches of grass in front of them.

She let out a big sigh. It didn't matter if Jody didn't understand her obsession with the show or the doll. It didn't even matter that their mom didn't understand Casey's burning need to get the Cowboy Cody doll.

None of it mattered because Casey planned to go over all

their heads. She was going directly to the big guy, Santa Claus himself. And since it was only two weeks until Christmas, she'd been extra good lately.

Cowboy Cody was as good as hers. She could feel it.

After Jody oooh'd and ahhh'd over some stuff in the store that didn't interest Casey at all as she continued to imagine waking up to Cowboy Cody under the tree, they finally moved on.

They'd just turned a corner when they ran head on into their mother. She was breathless and a little pink in the face. "You girls ready to go?"

Casey frowned. "Why do you look like you do after you get off your treadmill?"

Mom pressed her palms to her cheeks. "I guess I've been walking fast looking for you two."

Just shopping shouldn't make her mother out of breath. It was almost as if she'd been running around out in the parking lot or something. Her hair looked kind of windblown and even the tip of her nose was pink, like she'd been out in the cold.

Oh, well. It didn't matter if her mother wanted to act like a weirdo. Casey didn't know anyone in this store. It wasn't like they were at school where her mom's behavior could, and usually did, embarrass her.

Besides, Casey had other things to worry about. "Mom, can we go see Santa now?"

"Santa. Ha!" Jody's outburst earned her a look from their mother.

"Jody..."

Casey recognized the warning in her mother's tone. She'd been the recipient of it enough times herself. She couldn't help but smirk that this time it was all for Jody.

"Mom, I don't wanna go to the mall."

As they exited into the cold, Mom frowned at Jody's whining. "Well, Casey does and I want a picture of you both with Santa for the collection on the mantle."

Jody let out a huge sigh. "I'm too old to sit in Santa's lap."

"Then stand next him." Mom clicked the locks open for the SUV.

Since Jody got to sit up front because she was older, Casey crawled into the back seat. She strained her neck to see behind her. The far back of the car was packed with big plastic bags with the toy store's name on them. "Mom? What's in the back?"

Her mother's glare found Casey in the rearview mirror. "Casey Jean Harrington, turn around this instant or I'm telling Santa you don't do what you're told."

"Fine." She rolled her eyes.

It couldn't be for her anyway. Whatever was in those bags was huge and the only thing she wanted and had asked for was Cowboy Cody. He certainly didn't need a bag that big. It was probably stuff for the cousins she was forced to play with when they came for Christmas dinner.

She couldn't give much more thought to it now. She was going to get to see Santa and put in her live request to back up the letter she'd written to the North Pole a month ago, and she got to watch Jody be unhappy about going to the mall at the same time. It was a good day.

Hopefully, it was just the beginning of the best Christmas ever.

~ * ~

The sun streaming through the window next to the bed woke Casey Christmas morning.

Uh, oh. Wait. The sun was up?

Casey jumped out of bed. She'd planned on being up early. How had she overslept?

Not stopping long enough to put on slippers, she skidded in her socks into the hallway where she tripped along the wooden floor to the carpet runner. She slowed only long enough in her sprint to peek into Jody's room and make sure her sister was still sleeping.

The lump in the bed under the covers remained unmoving. Good! At least she hadn't slept later than her sister. Being first to get to the presents under the tree was almost as important as what was waiting there for her—Cowboy Cody.

Casey couldn't wait.

She barreled down the stairs and ran to her parents' bedroom, grabbing onto the doorframe to stop her momentum. "I'm opening presents."

"Casey, you wait for the rest of the family."

"Mom, no. Jody's still sleeping. I wanna open them now." It didn't matter if she was whining. Santa had come and gone. No need to be good now.

"Wait for your sister, and your father and me, Casey Jean, or I'll call Santa right now and tell him to come take your presents back." Her mom even went as far as reaching for the phone on the bedside table.

As if Santa would really come back. He'd be too tired for that. But just in case, Casey figured she'd give in. "Fine."

"Let the girl go and open her presents, Margaret." Her father's voice sounded sleepy and muffled as he lay facedown in his pillow.

"Thanks, Dad. Love you." She could have kissed her father, but first she had a cowboy to unwrap.

Without waiting to hear if her mother had agreed with her father, Casey ran to the living room and dove beneath the tree. With pine needles poking her in the back of the head, she began dragging presents out, flinging them to the side when they didn't have her name on them, or if they were the wrong size to be Cowboy Cody.

Finally she sat in the middle of the still-wrapped presents surrounding her, but the one she wanted wasn't there.

Maybe she'd missed it. She'd have to go back through them all again.

"What are you doing?" Jody yawned in the doorway while tying the belt on her pink and white polka-dot robe.

"Looking for my present."

"Maybe you didn't get any." The smirk on Jody's face was absolutely evil.

Casey had felt bad before that she'd flung one of Jody's

gifts so hard it had landed against the wall behind the tree, but not anymore.

"I did too get some, smarty. I got lots of presents." Just not one the size and shape of the Cowboy Cody box she'd seen on the toy store shelf.

Wait. Maybe Santa had put that box into a bigger box and then wrapped it. That would make sense. He wouldn't want her to guess what it was. He'd want her to be surprised.

Of course! Casey spun around to locate the big box she'd shoved to the side before. She spied it and dove, ripping at the paper the moment her hand made contact.

The torn wrappings revealed a picture of a pink oven and a smiling girl holding a tiny cake. Santa was very tricky putting Cowboy Cody inside this box—the box of something she hadn't asked for. Something she didn't even want.

Casey's short nails slid right over the thick clear tape sealing the cardboard closed. "I need something to cut this tape with. Mom! I need a scissor."

Her mother was up and in the kitchen. Casey could smell the coffee. Mom was always happier after drinking her coffee.

Camera in one hand and a scissor in the other, her mother came into the living room. "You need a scissor, *please…*"

"Please." Casey scrambled to her feet and grabbed for it.

She used the edge to slice through the tape and then yanked the sides of the box apart. She held her breath, waiting for her first sight of what she'd waited so long for…but it wasn't there.

Filling the whole box, held in place by white Styrofoam, was a pink plastic oven.

"Isn't that nice? Now you can bake cakes on your own. You always like to be in the kitchen while I'm baking." Casey's mother smiled and snapped a picture of her with the pink oven.

She was speechless. How could Santa do this to her? She'd been so good.

Her mother had to have gotten to him somehow. That

was the only explanation. Casey didn't want to bake little cakes in a plastic oven. She only hung out in the kitchen when her mother was baking because then she'd get to lick the icing off the beaters or eat the cookie dough raw.

Her mother was still looking at her, as if waiting for her to get excited about this. Even Jody had paused in her gift opening and was watching Casey.

"Um. I have to, uh, go to the bathroom."

"Okay, but come right back. There's more gifts that Grandma shipped up from Florida for you to open."

Casey nodded and scrambled to her feet. She had to get away from that pink thing sitting in the box that should have held the one item that would make her happy. She ran up the stairs and made a beeline to her room. Inside, she flung herself facedown onto the rumpled covers.

She didn't know how long she lay there, but all too soon Jody appeared in the doorway. "Mom wants you to come back downstairs so she can take pictures of us opening Grandma's gifts."

"I don't want to." Casey stayed facedown on her bed. "I was so good and I didn't get what I asked for."

"I know." The mattress dipped as Jody sat next to her. "I'm sorry you didn't get your doll."

Casey let out a snort. "No, you're not."

"Yeah, I am. I know you really wanted it. I don't get why you wanted it, but you did and I'm sorry you're sad." Jody's voice sounded pretty sincere, so Casey decided to believe she really meant it.

She turned over and tried to wipe the tears clinging to her lashes before Jody saw them. "Thank you."

"You wanna know a secret?"

She nodded. Maybe it would distract her from the biggest disappointment of her life.

Jody leaned in close. "Santa didn't give you that oven. Mom pretending to be Santa did."

Eyes and mouth wide open, Casey stared at Jody. "But—"

"Listen. Remember at the toy store when Mom told us to

shop by ourselves and then came running to find us and she was all out of breath? And then she yelled at you for looking at the packages in the back of the car? What do you think was in that bag?"

Realization hit. Casey sucked in a breath. "Santa is really Mom."

"Yeah. Sorry. I thought it was time for you to know."

Her entire world shifted. It all made sense now. Putting aside the disappointment that the man she'd believed in for eight years didn't exist, Casey clenched her teeth in anger. "Mom still knew I wanted Cowboy Cody. Why didn't she get him for me?"

Jody shrugged. "Mom usually gets me what she wants me to have, not what I really want. You think I asked for those rainbow striped rain boots? I wanted the ones with the leopard print on them."

Breath coming fast and with a violent mix of emotions warring inside her, Casey made a vow to herself. She'd grow up, get the best job in the world and then buy herself whatever she wanted for Christmas. And she'd never ever bake anything in that stupid oven, or in any other oven, for that matter. Ever!

CHAPTER ONE

Casey stood at the head of the long table in the World Bank's meeting room. She glanced down the two rows of businessmen seated on either side. Good thing she'd been there long enough to know them all by name, because at first glance they all looked exactly the same to an outsider.

Same navy blue suit. Same conservative tie. Same appropriate length hair gelled back to keep it in place. She even thought they might all be wearing the same cologne.

How sad was that? They didn't even smell different.

It was no wonder she was single. Not one of these guys had ever tempted her. How could they? Not one stood out from the rest.

She was drowning in a sea of sameness.

Their matching tablets were held poised in front of them on the conference table as they followed along with her presentation on their matching screens.

There was not one woman among them, save for herself. She stifled a sigh. The glass ceiling was still firmly in place. At least in this company.

How she'd managed to crack it, she didn't know. Hard work and determination played a part. That she'd never married and had kids, and in fact hadn't even dated in what felt like forever, meant she could work sixteen-hour days. That probably had helped her ascent in the ranks too.

It didn't matter. She was only twenty-eight. There was plenty of time for her to settle down, find a man, have some kids…later.

"Any questions, gentlemen?" She glanced at their faces again and saw them shake their heads in unison. Like synchronized swimmers in Italian suits. "All right, then. Thank you for your attention."

Outside of the Wall Street building, the Manhattan skyline was beginning to twinkle as dusk fell and lights flickered on. It was a beautiful sight. One she could enjoy from the window of her apartment as well—when she finally got home each night, usually carrying a bag of take-out food.

What did she feel like eating today? Sushi maybe? Though it was getting chilly. Autumn weather had set in fast. Maybe some *Udon* noodle soup from the sushi place.

Decision made, and with the room rapidly emptying of the clones who worked beneath her in the bank's corporate headquarters marketing department, Casey headed for her office. She could check her messages, then head out. Now that she had soup on the brain, her stomach was beginning to rebel from having skipped lunch.

A latte and a pastry did not a meal make. She'd have to remember that in the future as her stomach let out a loud grumble.

Good thing that hadn't happened during the presentation. She laughed to herself at the thought and glanced at the phone on her desk. There was no blinking red light to indicate she had a message. Excellent. That soup was getting closer by the second.

Grabbing her oversized bag, she was about to head out the door when the phone in her suit jacket pocket vibrated. She'd been so close… Casey sighed and pulled it out to look at the display.

It was a Manhattan area code, but she didn't recognize the

number. She hit the screen to answer. "Casey Harrington."

"Ms. Harrington. I'm so glad I got you. This is Madison at Smith and Brown."

She knew of Smith and Brown. They were headhunters. They called her a few times a year with some job offer or another.

"Yes, Madison. What can I do for you?" This call wasn't World Bank business or even important, so Casey figured she could walk while she talked. She always let the headhunters have their say, and then she'd politely tell them she wasn't interested. She was happy in her position at World Bank.

Casey gave the woman at the front desk a wave good bye and poked the button for the elevator.

"I have a position I think you'd be perfect for. Director of Marketing. Multi-national company but the corporate headquarters are located in Manhattan. Impressive benefits package and salary."

"That all sounds very nice, but I'm happy here at World Bank—"

"Ms. Harrington, I know other people from our firm have approached you in the past, but I've done my research and I truly think this position is different. I believe it's the one you've been waiting for."

Casey's eyebrows shot up. This was a new approach. But now that she thought about it, this Madison woman had never called before so she must also be new.

Either that, or Smith and Brown were pulling out the big guns, the upper level execs, to try to woo her. More intrigued with this new tactic, than in whatever this position was, Casey decided to hear the woman out, just to see where this conversation went. It would at least occupy her time while she walked to the restaurant.

"Exactly what research did you do, Madison, that makes you believe this is the position I've been waiting for?" Casey prepared herself to be amused by some bullshit.

"I've done research on you, Ms. Harrington."

"On me?" Okay, this was creepy. Casey started to feel like

she had a stalker.

"I know you volunteer. A lot. Not the normal stuff that looks good on paper or what's required for your position there at World Bank. You're a creative person and your choice of boards that you sit on, and charities that you support with your attendance at fundraisers, proves that."

"Uh, huh. You'll find most people in marketing are creative, Madison. It helps with the job."

"The Save the Wild Mustangs Foundation. The National Trust for Historic Preservation's campaign to preserve Main Street in small town America. The Cowboy Relief Fund for injured rodeo cowboys and clowns. These are not normal charities a banking executive who lives and works in Manhattan would gravitate toward."

So now she wasn't normal. Casey was pretty sure she should be insulted by that remark. Though Madison of Smith and Brown would be happy to know that Casey's family would agree that she wasn't normal. And the woman sure had done her research. "Is there a point to this?"

"Yes, there is. The position available is for the director of marketing at Maverick Western. They're a—"

"A western lifestyle retailer. I know. I get their catalog." Every year since she'd gotten her own apartment, Casey would wrap herself in the red and black plaid throw she'd bought from Maverick as she pawed through their Christmas catalog, dog earring pages of things she wanted.

She'd place orders for herself and her family, whether they liked it or not. Her apartment looked more like a cowboy camp than a city home.

Casey stomped down the excitement that rose unbidden within her.

"Yes, ma'am. That's the one. They're still family-owned. They've been in business for about a hundred years and the current owner, Jake Maverick, is looking to bring the company up to date with their marketing. He wants to insure the company's survival for the future."

"Why? Is the company in trouble?" Casey's throat

tightened.

She loved that catalog, from the pictures of the cowboys and the cattle on the ranch, to the tiny tabletop live evergreen trees they'd ship her overnight when she didn't have time to get a real Christmas tree for her apartment.

"No, I assure you they're quite stable financially, but they're smart enough to know there is an untapped market out there. A younger demographic. Internet users who won't take the time to read a paper catalog."

Casey nodded. "Exactly. They need an app so people can order on their tablets and smartphones. They should be on social media too, reinforcing their brand with those users."

"Exactly, Ms. Harrington." The smile in Madison's voice was clear.

Casey sighed. Damn, the woman was right. This was the position she'd been waiting for.

World Bank was a wonderful employer, but she was wasted here, her bottomless pool of creativity barely tapped by creating yet another boring ad campaign. The biggest excitement they'd had lately was getting a Hollywood B-lister to be their spokesperson in their television commercials.

But Maverick Western... Casey could be the one to bring them into the future. She could expose millions of new customers worldwide to the joys of shopping there. Introduce them to a new generation of shoppers.

"Ms. Harrington, there is one catch I feel I need to bring to your attention before we discuss any more details about the position."

A catch. Wasn't that always the way? "And what is that?"

"You might be aware that though the current corporate headquarters are in Manhattan, the company originated in Colorado on the family's ranch."

"Mm, hm. I believe that's where the catalog's exterior shots are taken."

"Yes, you're correct. It's a beautiful place. Well, Mr. Maverick insists that whoever takes this position spend a one week long training period, I guess you could call it, on the family ranch to get familiar with the company's philosophy and the lifestyle they represent. He feels very strongly about his head of marketing knowing his way of life."

"The cowboy code." Memories of every Saturday morning of her youth spent sitting in front of the Cowboy Cody show hit Casey. Wow. She hadn't thought about that show in years.

"Excuse me?" Madison's voice interrupted the thought.

"Um, nothing. So that would be the only stipulation? The training period on the ranch?"

"Yes. Of course there would be occasional travel as well. You'd be expected to fly to the ranch a couple of times a year. The usual travel for a position of this level."

"Mm, hm." It was nearly impossible to concentrate on what the woman was saying.

Visions of cowboys danced in Casey's head alongside ideas for a Maverick Western App for the millions of smartphones and tablet computers worldwide. And then there'd need to be a Facebook page, Instagram, Pinterest boards of decorating ideas, Snapchat, Twitter...

And of course website enhancements. There could be an interactive shopping list maybe, to help customers do their Christmas shopping—

"Can we meet to discuss the details?" Madison, sounding as excited as Casey felt, interrupted her mental marketing plans.

Casey pushed down the feeling, even as adrenaline pumped through her veins. It wasn't good to go into negotiations showing too much enthusiasm. Always best to play hard to get in these kinds of situations.

"I suppose I could squeeze in a meeting, just to hear the details."

"Wonderful. When and where? Name it and I'll be there. Our offices are in Manhattan not too far from yours."

Casey reached the Japanese restaurant and paused on the sidewalk as an insane impulse assaulted her. It was crazy but she couldn't stop herself from saying, "Are you free to meet me for dinner right now?"

CHAPTER TWO

"What the hell is this about? I don't understand." Bonner "Blue" Boyd stared at the paper in his hand, still not comprehending its meaning.

Putting a bowl of chili on the table in front of him, Mrs. Jones shot him a glare. "It's a memo. What's to understand? And don't cuss."

Dakota and Justus both snickered from their seats across the table from Bonner.

Mrs. Jones ran the Maverick household with an iron fist. No cowboy who worked on the ranch would dare to cross the housekeeper, who'd worked there since before Bonner was born.

"Yes, ma'am. I'm sorry." Suitably reprimanded, he still took the opportunity to shoot Dakota and Justus a dirty look for laughing at his expense. "But what I don't understand is why I got it. Why send me a memo when he could just call me? Or ask me to come talk to him in person?"

Bonner put the piece of paper down next to his dish and picked up the spoon, digging into the bowl of steaming hot food like a starving man. He and the two younger cowboys had been out fixing fences on the ranch since sun-up with no break, so he sure felt like a starving man.

"That is pretty strange, Blue, you getting that paper. 'Cause none of us were all too sure you could read." Dakota chuckled at his own joke and elbowed Justus, who joined in the laughter.

Old Mrs. Jones slapped both men in the back of their heads, a move Bonner probably enjoyed watching a bit too much. "You two be nice. And you, Bonner, know Jake's doctor told him he has to start taking things easier. That's why he's been having that assistant in the New York office handle more of the things he used to do himself. He's finally letting someone else take care of some of the business details for him and it's about damn time too. At his age he needs to slow down. It's bad enough he drove himself into the city today to some business meeting."

"So now I'm getting memos. Because of his dam—dang assistant." Bonner corrected his language just in time to avoid getting smacked, but he couldn't suppress a sigh.

He was a cattle rancher, for Christ's sake. Ranchers didn't get memos. They also shouldn't have to deal with business details…at least not ones that involved huge international corporations like the kind Maverick Western had grown into since it was founded by the Maverick family a hundred years ago.

Sure, Bonner could easily calculate the value of the Maverick's four hundred head herd. Yeah, he could figure how much fencing to buy for repairs on the over three thousand acre ranch. He knew when to cut the hay field for the highest yield. He could read the weather and knew when to drive the herd to the summer pasture for grazing and when to bring them back down again to the ranch for the winter.

Those kinds of details he could handle in his sleep. But this… He glared down again at the corporate letterhead on his memo.

"What's it say, Blue?" Justus glanced at the paper as he reached for the basket of cornbread in the middle of the table.

"There's some guy just got hired in the New York office and I'm supposed to take this," Bonner looked at the paper and located the name, "Casey Harrington and teach him everything about life on the ranch for a doggone week."

Justus's eyes opened wide, before his face split into a grin. "State rodeo champion Blue Boyd playing babysitter for a corporate big wig."

"For a solid week." Dakota shook his head. "Too funny. I'd pay good money to see that."

"That's the beauty of it, Dakota. We won't have to. It'll all be happening right here on the ranch, free of charge." Justus continued to look too happy at Bonner's expense.

"First off, I'm the *former* state champion. My rodeo days are in the past." And Bonner wished they'd stay there. "And I'm sure you'll both be too busy doing my share of the work while I'm babysitting this guy to have any time to be amused."

That knocked the grin off the faces of both ranch hands, but Bonner still had to wonder what the hell he was supposed to do with some city slicker shadowing him for a week. Jake Maverick had really lost his mind this time.

Looking a whole lot more serious now at the prospect of having to work harder, Dakota frowned. "When's this new marketing dude getting here?"

Good question. Bonner skimmed over the page of print and stalled at a date. "Um, what day is it?"

"Monday."

He rolled his eyes at Justus. "I know it's Monday. I meant what's the date."

"Oh, um…" Justus glanced at Dakota, who shrugged in response.

This just proved they were cowboys and not corporate folk. Unless he was headed to an auction or a rodeo, the exact date didn't matter all that much here at the ranch.

Bonner's world revolved around the seasons—calving season, cutting season—important stuff like that. Little numbered squares on a calendar didn't matter all that much.

"Wait. The date's on my cell, I think." Dakota whipped his phone out of his jeans pocket and squinted at it for a bit. "Here it is. October 24th."

Both kids watched Bonner as he raised a brow. "Well, then that would mean this Casey Harrington person is arriving today."

Mrs. Jones came through the door. "I could have told you that. I had to set up one of the bedrooms."

"Oh? You get a memo too?" Bonner glanced at her as she put a pitcher full of water down.

"Me? A memo?" She let out a snort of a laugh. "He knows better."

As Mrs. Jones disappeared into the kitchen, Bonner scowled. Memos. City folk. Marketing. Things sure weren't like they used to be.

"How's he getting here?"

While downing a swallow of water, Bonner shrugged at Dakota's question.

"Got me. Not my problem." That part wasn't in Bonner's memo so he picked up his spoon again and scraped the bottom of the bowl to get the last remnants of chili, then put it down on the table with a clunk. "You boys 'bout done? We got work to finish."

They had better get to it. The pressure was on since it seemed, like it or not, Bonner's babysitting duties would begin shortly.

CHAPTER THREE

Yampa Valley Regional Airport in Colorado wasn't as horrifying as the name first implied.

Sure there was no air traffic control tower. And yes, Casey had to navigate a set of air stairs to deplane and then brave the icy wind as she crossed the tarmac to get to the terminal, but at least she'd flown in from Denver International on a Boeing rather than some little crop duster, which had been what she'd feared.

Now, in her rental car, she tried not to panic as the navigation's computerized voice told her she was driving on an unrecognized route.

She glanced at her cell phone. No signal.

A woman alone, driving after sunset on an unrecognized route with no cell reception—this situation had all the makings of a bad horror movie. Casey pushed that thought out of her head. This was no time to panic.

Besides, she had a nearly full tank of gas. If worst came to worst, she'd turn around, drive back to the nearest town and call the ranch from a landline.

She should be able to get in touch with the Maverick place somehow. Jake Maverick ran a multi-national corporation, and this was the twenty-first century. Though looking around her now at the deserted landscape, it sure didn't look like it.

Casey fought back the panic. She'd thought she'd be okay when she heard it was less than an hour's drive from the airport to the Colorado/Wyoming border where the Maverick ranch was located, but she'd seen nothing but open road for miles now. Even as the GPS read-out said she had less than three miles to her destination, she still saw nothing.

She'd traveled all over Europe without incident for her job with the bank, but this country road was about to break her. Casey refused to think this career move was a mistake, though the sick feeling in her gut began to disagree with her stubborn mindset.

What had she been thinking accepting this position? She'd probably never been within a hundred miles of a cowboy or a cow, and here she was leaving a good job to try and market the cowboy lifestyle for Maverick Western.

What if Jake Maverick took one look at her and realized she was a fraud?

Then again, her college marketing professor had once said marketing was marketing. It didn't matter what you were selling because it wasn't really about the product, it was about how it made the consumer feel.

Casey knew well how Maverick Western products made her feel, from the flannel pajamas packed in her suitcase to the cast iron skillet she'd had to have but never used, stored in the cabinet below the stove in her New York apartment.

She had the skills to expand the market, hitting demographics missed by the current catalog and website the company relied on now. She could do this job and she'd kick ass at it. She had to, because there was no going back. World Bank hadn't been too happy about her departure.

The sick feeling in her gut returned.

Then the car's headlights hit a high gate over the road she'd been blindly traveling on for the past few miles. Casey slowed to a crawl and flipped on the brights, illuminating the letters that spelled Maverick. She blew out a long breath.

What she stared at now was more than just an entrance gate to a ranch. It was like a divine sign from the heavens. Somehow it equaled hope. If she could make it to the ranch alone, she could make it in the job. She'd found the ranch and now all she had to do was stick it out for a week while not disappointing the boss.

She'd worry about that tomorrow. For tonight she needed a bathroom, something to eat and maybe a good stiff drink, possibly not in that order.

Casey pulled ahead with newfound enthusiasm, until she realized that once again she'd driven miles and there was still no house in sight.

She began to doubt herself again.

Had she missed a turn? Or even the house in the dark? Surely there'd be some lights on. Someone was supposed to be home to meet her. She glanced at the GPS. That was no help. It had told her she'd reached her destination miles ago and still had her on an unmarked route.

Stupid technology. They had the know-how to get a man to the space station but they couldn't come up with a GPS that could tell you where you were in Colorado.

Was she even still on Maverick property? This was so far removed from her life in Manhattan, or even her childhood in the suburbs in Connecticut, she was having trouble wrapping her mind around it.

There was really nothing else to do but forge ahead. She had to see something eventually, but who would have thought there could possibly be this many miles of undeveloped land left in the United States?

Land was a hot commodity. Try buying even one acre of it in certain communities in the metro New York area and it could cost upwards of a million dollars. Not here. Apparently there was plenty of land left on the Colorado-Wyoming border.

With her hands starting to cramp from gripping the steering wheel so tight, Casey crept along with her eyes peeled for any sign of civilization. Then she saw it, two glowing eyes appeared before her from out of the darkness.

A yelp escaped her lips. She slammed on the brakes. Her body rocked toward the windshield from the momentum. "What the hell?"

The animal, larger than she was comfortable being near, stared at the car for a second and then bolted across the road. It could have been a deer, or an elk or a damn antelope for all she knew. Were there moose in Colorado? The only experience she had with wild animals in the city were pigeons and the occasional squirrel.

This was crazy. Her heart pounded. If she could disengage her fingers from their death-grip on the steering wheel, she was sure her hands would be shaking. She was going to die, here on an unrecognized route somewhere in Colorado.

Eventually someone would find her body, dry and shriveled, signal-less cell phone clutched in her hand as she sat in the driver's seat of the mid-sized rental car, the GPS still saying she'd reached her destination.

Casey didn't cry. Nope. She hadn't since she'd been a child. There was no place for tears for a female trying to make it in the male-dominated corporate world.

But tonight, tired, hungry and lost alone in the dark, she felt the first tears in years begin to sting her eyes. Then she had to shield her eyes from the blinding glare of headlights shining directly at her.

The pick-up truck, looking huge compared to her car, came to a stop and the driver's side door swung open. Not sure whether to be relieved or frightened, Casey felt in the dark for the controls on her door. She confirmed the doors were locked, then cracked the window open just enough to talk through.

The car was still in drive. If whoever was in that truck was dangerous, she'd just floor it. She'd be a mile away by the time he got back into the truck, turned it around and tried to follow.

Lit by her headlights, a figure climbed down from the high vehicle. Big and tall, he raised his hand and tipped his brown felt cowboy hat down so it shielded his eyes from the glare.

Her heart picked up speed but she wasn't sure if it was from fear, or the fact that this man, by all appearances a real-live walking talking cowboy, was coming right at her.

In boots and worn faded jeans, with a jacket opened to reveal a blue shirt, he kind of swaggered, which only added to the whole cowboy look of him. As did the black and white dog that leapt from the vehicle and, tail wagging, trailed along at his heels.

He reached the side of the car and, hands shoved into his front jean's pockets, he leaned down to peer into the window. "You lost?"

Just the deep timber of those two words, spoken with the drawl of a true cowboy, cut directly through her. Casey could barely breathe. This man was the personification of her first childhood love—Cowboy Cody and the Cowboy Code.

"Um, I didn't think so when I saw the sign, but now I've been driving for so long I'm afraid I might be and the GPS is no help. It doesn't even recognize the road and my cell won't work." Compared to this man of few words, her longwinded answer sounded ridiculous.

He probably thought she was some kind of idiot.

Her cowboy savior rubbed his thumb and forefinger over the closely cropped beard on his chin. "Well, tell me where you need to get to. Maybe I can help."

Helpful and logical. Of course he'd be able to help. He probably knew right where they were.

"I'm trying to get to the Maverick ranch." She watched as beneath the brim of his hat, his eyebrows rose sharply. That action made her feel like she needed to explain herself. "They're expecting me. I'm staying there for the next week. Mr. Maverick invited me." Casey kept adding on facts, hoping to jog him into saying something, anything, as he stared at her with a strange expression on his face. "I work for him. Or I will after this week. He just hired me."

Didn't he believe her? Was she trespassing on someone else's land? Did they shoot trespassers out here?

"*You're* Casey Harrington?" A frown creased his brow as he blew out a long slow breath.

Oh thank God. He knew her name. She must be in the right place. He wasn't going to shoot her, or call the sheriff, or whatever. Though she did find it strange he seemed so shocked at her appearance since he knew she was coming.

"Yes, I am." She nodded. When he still didn't seem all that receptive she added, "Sorry if I'm late."

He shook his head, a slow motion accompanied by a short laugh that sounded more like a sigh. "No problem. Follow me."

His last word was spoken as he turned on his heel and, dog in tow, headed back to the truck.

"Well, all righty then." Casey spoke to no one as she raised the window and watched Mr. Talkative get into the truck.

Not so verbose here in Colorado, were they? She expected cowboys to be smooth talkers. All "Shucks, darlin', aren't you a pretty little filly" or "Yes, ma'am, it would surely be my honor to help out a lady in need," or something charmingly Western like that.

That's what she got for forming an opinion about an entire group of men before getting to know them—disappointed.

This was probably the reason she was still single. It didn't matter whether the guy was a CEO on Wall Street or a cowboy on the Wyoming border, men were men, and they always seemed to let her down because no one could ever live up to her overly high expectations. She'd have to remember, Cowboy Cody and his cowboy code were fiction.

Lesson learned, she followed the truck after it made a U-turn and headed up the dark road that led God only knew where.

Welcome to the Wild West.

CHAPTER FOUR

After a restless night's sleep, Bonner pulled his truck up to the main house and put it into park. The sight that greeted him had his hand slipping off the gearshift.

Their visitor was awake? At sunrise? He'd figured he wouldn't see her until the noon meal.

This woman was full of surprises, the first being that she was a woman. He'd assumed Casey was a *he* and it turned out she was most definitely a *she*. He glanced at her on the front porch now.

Yup, Casey Harrington was all woman, with chestnut hair that cascaded over her shoulders and big green eyes; not to mention curves a man could get lost in. She held a coffee cup as she stood gazing at the mountains in the distance. The bulky white sweater that came to past her waist didn't do shit to hide how her dark blue jeans cupped the perfectly rounded cheeks of her butt.

When Bonner could yank his attention away from that tempting asset—and the thought of how nice it would be to get to know that part of her a little better—he was surprised yet again. She was wearing cowboy boots.

Last night when he'd helped carry her matching luggage

into the house, all *three* pieces of it, she'd been in some suit kind of thing. City girl to the bone, right down to her fancy cell phone that apparently didn't work around these parts, according to her rant in the car.

He hadn't stuck around to learn more last night. He'd dumped her and her baggage with Mrs. Jones and taken off to deal with this new bit of information. He was not only babysitting a city girl for the next week, but one who had him waking up from a dream starring her last night.

How was he supposed to deal with this?

At least this morning she was actually dressed appropriately for a day on the ranch. She wouldn't be tiptoeing around the cow manure in high heels. But did she have to look so damn good in jeans? Even if they did look like they'd just come off the shelf of some overpriced city store, they sure did the job of drawing his gaze right to where it shouldn't be.

Dammit.

He swung the truck door wide and got out.

She broke her gaze away from the landscape and turned to smile at him as he climbed the stairs onto the porch. "Good morning."

"Morning." Bonner tipped his hat.

Her gaze swept to where his truck was parked. "Where's your dog?"

Hm, she sure was observant. He'd always thought city folk were blind to their surroundings, being as their heads were usually up their asses and all.

"Back at the bunkhouse with the boys. She'll be along later. I didn't expect to see you out so early." More accurately, Bonner had been hoping she'd sleep the day away so he'd have to spend less time babysitting her—and less time being tempted.

"I'm still on East Coast time. I would've been at my desk by now, probably on a conference call with the London office if I were still at my old job at World Bank."

"Ah." He nodded. That made more sense. He hadn't

considered the difference between Mountain and Eastern Time, or the possibility of London offices. Jeez. It all seemed like another universe.

"This is…just amazing." She shook her head while gazing again at the sunrise. "There are no words. When I got here last night in the dark, I had no idea how beautiful it was. I never imagined this."

Again impressed that this New York woman could appreciate the beauty of the country, Bonner took the time to glance at the colored hues starting to already disappear as the sun rose higher above the horizon. He saw the sun rise every morning over these mountains and had since he was born.

It sure was a sight. He supposed he should appreciate it a little more. This city girl was a reminder that not everybody was as lucky.

"Have you ever been to New York?" she asked.

Bonner shook his head. "Nope." And he had no desire to.

"Well, I can tell you, there's nothing there that compares to this."

He shot a sideways look at Casey again as she continued to stare at the surroundings. The tip of her nose was beginning to turn pink from the nip in the air. She didn't seem to care as she cupped the coffee mug in both hands but didn't drink. It reminded him why he was here, besides to pick up his latest assignment from Jake Maverick.

"I'm gonna head on in and get some of that for myself along with some breakfast." Bonner tipped his chin toward her mug.

"I'll come in with you. We can go over today's agenda."

Agenda?

First memos. Now agendas. City girl may come with a nice ass, but she also brought a hell of a lot of changes along with her. Bonner didn't like change.

Opening the door, he stepped to the side to allow her to go in first. That earned him a wide smile from Miss Corporate Marketing Director as she said, "Thank you."

He nodded and then decided to break the bad news to her.

"I, uh, don't really have an agenda. I just figured you'd hang around with me as I do what I normally do."

They walked to the dining room where Bonner saw their guest had already been busy. Her bag and one of those new kind of flat computer things, no bigger across than a piece of paper, sat on the table.

She put her coffee down and picked it up.

"That's fine. What do you normally do?" She waited, poised to take notes, he guessed.

Now that the pressure was on and she'd captured him in that emerald gaze of hers, he'd be damned if he could name one thing he did there at the ranch. "Uh, well—"

"Morning, Bonner." Mrs. Jones arrived with a platter full of eggs and bacon and saved him from having to answer.

"Mornin'." Thank God for small favors. Now with the food on the table, he'd have time to think what to say to her. He reached for the serving spoon and then remembered they had a guest. "Ma'am?"

Bonner moved the spoon around to her side of the platter, just as Dakota and Justus burst through the front door.

This was going to be good. They'd been at the bunkhouse when their guest had arrived last night, and Bonner hadn't told them about the new development yet. He spun in his seat and waited for their entrance into the dining room.

Justus stopped dead in the doorway and Dakota, who hadn't been watching where he was going, plowed head-on into the back of him.

Bonner grinned as their reaction didn't disappoint. They fell over their own feet just from seeing Casey seated at the table.

"Justus, Dakota, meet Miss Casey Harrington, our guest from corporate headquarters." Enjoying it all, Bonner grinned broader. Then a brilliant idea struck him. "She was just asking what we do around here. Why don't you two tell her?"

There. Now Bonner could eat his breakfast while it was still hot, and get to watch these two young cowboys blush in the presence of an attractive woman when they'd definitely come in expecting to find a man.

Bonner considered her looks again himself. She was attractive in a way that stopped a man in his tracks and made him look twice. But beyond that, she was tough and as strong-willed as any man. He could tell just by looking at her. Even in the short time he'd spent with her that quality shone through.

Aside from when he'd found her along the road last night, flustered because she thought she was lost, she wasn't a shrinking violet. Hell, she had to be capable or Jake Maverick wouldn't have looked twice at her for his company.

She was tough as a man, yet she somehow managed to be hot as hell and all woman.

Meanwhile, he'd gone to bed and woken up thinking about her even though she was the opposite of everything he usually found attractive in a female.

Well, except for the ass. He was definitely an ass man and she had an exceptionally nice one. But as far as the rest, yeah, as different as night and day.

The girls he'd dated were usually barrel racers, large animal vets, stock contractors, a barmaid or two. They didn't wear a business suit and sit at a desk behind a computer running large companies.

Strangely, those girls never made him react with one glance the way Casey Harrington had this morning on the porch.

"Miss Casey, can I get you some more coffee?" Justus abandoned his seat before she even had time to answer.

Dakota stood. "I was going to get her more coffee."

After scooping up a generous helping, Bonner dug into his plate full of eggs and watched the two boys jostle for Casey's attention as Mrs. Jones came through the kitchen door.

The housekeeper shot both young cowboys a look. "Sit down, both of you. I've got the coffee and I'll pour it if she wants it. Jeez. Ask them for help and they grumble and moan. But a pretty girl shows up and it's all helpful manners."

Casey grinned. "Thank you, Mrs. Jones. I'd love more

coffee."

So this was how it was going to be. Bonner glanced at the object of their obsession as she smiled.

Casey was young enough that these youngin's figured they had a shot with her. She was definitely younger than Bonner's thirty-three, but not by too much he figured.

He would have to dispel any notions these two had at first opportunity. Nobody was going to touch Jake Maverick's new corporate executive. The old man would definitely not be happy if that happened.

Besides, if there was going to be any touching happening around here, it sure as hell wasn't going to be between this hot woman and either one of these two rookies.

Seniority had to count for something at this operation. Experience too. Bonner smothered a grin thinking how he could best use his many years of experience on Miss Casey. And he sure as hell wasn't thinking about his years of ranching experience either. But that wouldn't be happening. There was no room for mixing business and pleasure around here.

While Bonner bit into a crackling piece of bacon, he watched as Justus and Dakota stepped all over each other telling her all the things they did on the ranch. This wasn't too bad at all, since they were doing the work for him.

However, it was Bonner who Casey would be shadowing for the next week.

He watched her as she nodded politely while Justus and Dakota talked. The view was damn nice. Creamy white skin. Bright eyes. His attention dropped to her mouth as she nibbled on a piece of bacon.

His mind went to bad places as he imagined those cupid's bow-shaped lips involved in other activities involving him.

Not good. He was going to have to keep his own libido in check. He reminded himself his hands-off-the-executives policy wasn't just for Justus and Dakota.

Shame. Damn shame.

Casey turned her attention toward Bonner and he realized

she'd spoken to him. Shit. "Uh, pardon?"

"I said I was hoping to get to meet Mr. Maverick. Is he here on the ranch?"

Bonner nodded. "He should be down soon. He gets up later and later nowadays. He's getting up there in years."

"Speak for yourself."

All eyes turned toward the doorway at the gruff voice as Jake Maverick arrived in the room. Even at his age, which was on the downward side of eighty now, his was a commanding presence.

Bonner grinned at the man who was more family than a boss to him. "Morning."

"Yeah, yeah, good morning to you too." Jake shot a scowl in Bonner's direction then turned to the lady seated at the table. "Miss Harrington, nice to finally meet you."

She rose and extended her hand, all business and corporate-like. "The pleasure is all mine, sir."

Jake shook her hand. "Please. Sit. Finish your breakfast." He moved to the empty chair at the head of the table. "My apologies for not being here yesterday when you arrived. I had some business to take care of in the city. I didn't get back until late."

"Quite all right. I got here after dark myself. Thank goodness Mr. Boyd here was driving by at the right time. I was nearly lost on the ranch. I never expected it to be so big." Her eyes grew wide.

Bonner had to smile. She hadn't been lost at all. She was on the drive headed straight for the main house. She just hadn't gone far enough.

"Well then I owe Bonner a thanks. Can't have my new director of marketing lost on my own ranch, now can I?"

"We could have come looking for you if Blue hadn't found you." Justus jumped in.

"Blue?" Casey glanced from Justus to Bonner.

Bonner sighed. He liked to avoid talking about his old rodeo days. The past was best left buried. "It's just an old nickname. It's what my father used to call me when I was little."

"I call you that." Justus glanced up from his plate.

Dakota nodded. "Me too. So do all the guys. And that's the name you rode under when you were rodeoing. Blue Boyd. I used to come see you compete when I was little."

Great. Just what Bonner needed, a reminder of how much older he was than these two.

"Rodeo?" Casey spun toward Bonner. "You're in the rodeo?"

"Not anymore." And that was all Bonner was going to say about that, even if Casey's eyes had lit up at the prospect.

What interest did a city girl have with rodeo anyway? He noticed Jake watching the exchange with an amused expression and decided to bring this conversation back to business, where it belonged. "So, boss, any special instructions for me today?"

Jake let out a bark of a laugh. "Since when do you ever ask me for instructions?"

Since he'd been told the new Maverick director of marketing would be up his butt for a week. Bonner decided he shouldn't say that. Instead he shrugged. "I was just wondering if you wanted me to cover anything in particular with our special guest, is all."

Casey turned toward Jake. "I want to see everything. I think you're right. It'll help me better craft the tone of the social media campaign if I can be totally immersed in daily life here at the ranch."

Oh, Bonner could show her *everything*, all right. Gladly. Glancing at his boss, the man who'd been like a grandfather to him from the day he was born, he gave himself a mental slap.

Not gonna happen. He had too much respect for Jake and Maverick Western to indulge his baser instincts and diddle with the new hire.

"Well, today the boys and I are going to see which cows are open."

Her perfectly shaped eyebrows rose. "Open for what?"

Justus and Dakota both let out snickers. Bonner shot them a look before turning back to Casey. "Open means they're not pregnant." He put it in the simplest terms he could since she was a city girl.

"Oh." Impossibly, her brows shot higher. And did her cheeks turn a bit pink? "And, um, how do you determine that?"

Now, even Bonner couldn't control his smile. "It's probably best if we wait and not tell you that right now."

"Why not?" A deep frown creased Casey brow.

Tough city girl didn't like being told no. Bonner tucked that information away for later.

Justus answered, "Because you're still eating."

The two younger men chuckled as Mrs. Jones came through the doorway carrying a bowl and a mug.

"Don't scare her away on the first day." She put the steaming bowl in front of Jake.

He scowled down at it. "Oatmeal again?"

"You know what the doctor said. Oatmeal and decaf coffee, and I don't want to hear anything more about it." That said, Mrs. Jones spun on her heel and was gone, back to the kitchen.

The minute she cleared the doorway, Jake reached out and snagged Bonner's mug.

"Hey!" Bonner frowned.

"Here. Take mine." Jake slid his own mug of decaf toward him, as if it would replace the coffee he'd stolen. "I'll eat this wallpaper paste she feeds me, but I refuse to give up real coffee. You gonna turn me in?"

Jake's snowy white brow rose.

Bonner laughed. "No, sir."

"Good boy." Jake's gaze perused the table. "Hand me a piece of bacon too. Quick, before she comes back."

With a glance at the kitchen door to make sure the coast was clear, Bonner shook his head and did as asked. "Don't blame me when you fall over dead one day."

"I'll outlive you boys. Just wait and see." Jake winked at

Casey.

She smiled. "I'm starting to envy you all your life here."

Jake paused with the spoon of oatmeal in mid-air. "Oh, really? And why is that, Miss Harrington?"

"It seems like much more fun working here than in the offices in New York."

Jake laughed. "Come back to me a week from now. We'll see if you still think so."

She cocked a brow, making her look like a vixen…and Bonner really needed to stop looking at her like that. He wasn't into torturing himself. Wanting something he couldn't have would be just that. Torture.

Besides, who's to say she'd even look twice at him. What would a city girl want with an old ranch hand like him?

"Is that a challenge, Mr. Maverick?" she asked.

Jake pressed his lips together and nodded. "Could be. You up to it?"

Bonner shook his head and watched them square off against each other. Casey and Jake couldn't be more different, yet it seemed they had one thing in common because the old man never could resist a challenge.

"Of course, I'm up for it. I'm a New Yorker."

"That's exactly what I'm worried about, darlin'."

Her expression wavered and for the first time today, Casey didn't ooze cool confidence. Instead, she looked a little worried.

This little visit was proving to be more interesting than Bonner had imagined, in so many ways.

CHAPTER FIVE

"So, they run the cows into a squeeze chute one at a time." Bonner stood next to her in the cold morning air.

"Okay." Casey watched as the two young cowboys accompanied by a barking Misty, the cattle dog, did as Bonner described, herding a cow between the metal rails.

"Then the vet feels her uterus to see if she's been bred and is carrying."

As the vet lubed his arm from hand to shoulder, Casey began to figure out the purpose of the extremely long plastic glove he'd put on. Her eyes opened wide.

No, he couldn't possibly...but then he did. The vet lifted the cow's tail and then his entire arm disappeared inside the cow who—immobilized in the chute—didn't have a whole lot it could do about it.

Casey cringed. "Wow."

Beside her, Bonner laughed. "We need to know which cows aren't bred. Rectal palpitation isn't as reliable as blood tests or ultrasounds, but it's the quickest and cheapest way to separate the cows that are bred from the ones that aren't."

"I guess so." She swallowed hard as the first victim was released from the chute and the next one was subjected to the vet's inspection.

Jeez, couldn't they all just pee on a stick and see if it turned pink? That seemed a hell of a lot easier than this, for everyone involved. As the vet did his thing the cow let out a short moo of protest.

A shudder ran through Casey and she didn't think it was from the cold air.

Glancing over, she noticed Bonner smirk. Casey turned her attention to him—a much more pleasant sight than what was happening behind the metal rails of the chute.

Damn, he was hot. Even though most of his sentences contained only a handful of single syllable words, they were delivered in a low, slow way that made her insides heat.

After all these years, it seemed she still hadn't gotten over her cowboy obsession. It was well ingrained by her eight-year-old self's unquenched desire for Cowboy Cody.

It didn't help that the man next to her looked uncannily like him, right down to the intense blue eyes beneath the brim of the cowboy hat…the exact eyes that were focused on her now.

He expected her to fail at this ranching stuff. For her to run crying back to the city. She could tell that just by the ever-present smirk and the way he watched her.

That was not going to happen. Casey Harrington didn't give up.

On the other hand, she might well be fired if she didn't prove herself to Jake Maverick. She knew she could do this job. She just had to make sure he knew that too. And if not blinking an eye at this insane cow rectum inspection was what Bonner Blue Boyd needed to make a favorable report to Mr. Maverick, then so be it.

She folded her arms and leaned back against the fence, settling in for a long haul. "So, how many are there to test?"

"Couple hundred."

Her eyes opened wide. "A couple hundred? This is going to take all day."

The shock of that shook her resolve to handle whatever

Bonner and the Maverick ranch threw at her.

"Yup." The man of few words was observing her reaction again.

Fine. Let him. She forced herself to look unfazed.

"Blue! You gonna help us or what?" Justus was out of breath as he yelled over. It was his job to slam the gate shut behind the cow once it was in the chute. He, Dakota and the dog were scrambling to keep up with the veterinarian, who seemed to be able to check the cows as fast as the cowboys could herd them into the chute.

"You two can handle this just fine on your own." Bonner leaned back against the fence next to her and crossed his arms.

Justus made a face but didn't argue. The kid had other things to worry about since the barking dog was running a cow right at him. The near trampling might have helped with his compliance.

Casey watched with interest. "You enjoy bossing them around, don't you?"

"No." Bonner glanced at her with a frown. "Young cowboys are like young horses. They need a strong hand. I was no different at that age. We're all cut from the same piece of leather."

That was one hell of a good line. She could use that in the Maverick marketing. She wasn't sure exactly how but she would. Somehow. Somewhere.

Casey pulled out her smart phone and opened the note application. Her fingers flew over the keyboard.

"What are you doing?" A crease knit above Bonner's ice blue eyes.

"Writing that down."

"Writing what down?"

"What you said. About being cut from the same piece of leather." She glanced up at him again and was tempted to laugh at how deep the furrow between his brows had grown.

"Why?" His frown turned into more of a scowl.

"Because I'd like to refer back to it for my marketing plan.

Lines like that, right out of a cowboy's mouth, will lend flavor. Believability. Buyers will love it. Besides, you heard Mr. Maverick. He's concerned I'm from the city. I have to prove to him I can market a western corporation or I could very well find myself on the unemployment line."

Bonner shook his head. "He wouldn't have hired you if he didn't think you could do the job."

Wow. Phone still in her hand, Casey turned her full attention to Bonner. "Thank you. It means a lot to hear you say that."

"It's the truth. From what I've seen so far, you'll be fine." Bonner shrugged and gazed at the action as the cowboys continued to herd the cows to the vet.

Casey had received lots of compliments from many men throughout her career. Some sincere, some pure flattery, but none of them had made her want to jump the man saying it. Not like Bonner's plainly spoken words just had.

She realized they were in the midst of an awkward silence as he glanced back at her. She tried to talk her woman parts out of inviting Bonner's man parts over to play.

Damn, she felt like a horny teenager again, only the object of her attention was no boy. He was all grown up and all man.

Trying to get control of herself, she scrambled for a safe topic. She glanced down at her phone. No signal.

"I just wish I had some kind of connection. I can get one, maybe two bars on my cell if I lean it against the window of my bedroom. Otherwise, it's pretty much worthless. My tablet's not picking up a signal either. I feel cut off from everything I need to do my job. Do you have cell service out here?"

"Here? Don't know. Never checked." He pulled out his phone and glanced at the readout. "Nope."

"No? Aren't you worried?"

"'Bout what?"

"What if one of you gets hurt?" Casey's mind spun with the possibilities, each more horrid than the last.

What if they were on horseback, far from the ranch, farther from help, with no cell phone signal and no vehicle to take them to the hospital?

He shrugged. "There're usually the three of us working together. If one gets hurt, one will go for help and the other can stay to tend to him."

"But...to have no means of communication." She'd panicked the one time her phone's battery had gone dead, and she was in a taxi in midtown Manhattan at the time.

Bonner glanced at her and shook his head. "You city folk are too dependent on your gadgets. Ranchers a hundred years ago didn't have cell phones. Hell, most ranch hands twenty years ago didn't."

Feeling a bit insulted by the city folk comment, even if she did wonder sometimes if she was becoming obsessed with technology, Casey planted her hands on her hips. He couldn't possibly be as complacent about this as he pretended. "Then why do you have a cell phone?"

"They were giving them away for free when you signed up." He shrugged. "Works just fine in the bunkhouse. It's useful sometimes."

"Oh really, like when?"

"Well, last year I was at a stock auction and I saw this little black and white Shetland pony. The old man had just had a new great-grand-baby, so I called to ask if he wanted me to pick it up for him to give as a baby gift."

The old man. Casey laughed. "There is just so much about that sentence that sounded insane to me I can't even begin to tell you."

This guy was the real deal, all right. Horseman. Cattleman. Cowboy. Lover?

Mm, wouldn't that be nice.

"Why? What's strange about it?" Bonner turned toward Casey, an expression of confusion on his face.

"First, you talk about buying a horse like you're picking up a loaf of bread at the grocery store. But more importantly, a pony? As a baby gift?"

Bonner shrugged again, something he seemed to do a lot around her. Apparently her city folk questions left him without answers.

"I was on a horse before I could walk."

Cowboy to the bone. And boy did she ache to get to know every inch of him better. She took him in from the felt of his hat to the leather of his boots.

On a horse before he could walk—that skill at riding horses had to transfer to other activities. Like those that happened in the bedroom. No? All that hip motion and thigh power...

"Mm. I have no doubt." The comment came out a bit more sultry-sounding than she'd intended.

Bonner cleared his throat. "Look, Miss Harrington—"

"Call me Casey."

He let out a huff of a breath. "Miss Casey—" Not exactly what she'd meant but it certainly had its charm. "—I realize I may not be the sharpest tool in the shed, but I know a few things. I know cattle and I know women."

This was pure cowboy gold.

The woman in her wanted to take a step closer to better absorb the cowboy aura of him. While the marketing director in her itched to write it all down, but she was too fascinated by what he was saying.

She didn't want to risk distracting him from finishing so she nodded. "Okay."

"What I'm trying to say is, I don't mix business with pleasure." Bonner shook his head. "As much as I'd like to, and believe me...I'd like to."

As much as he'd like to.

Embarrassment that her attraction to him was so obvious he'd found it necessary to comment on it warred with her glee that he felt it too.

Her chest tightened at the knowledge he felt the attraction between them, even though the rest was not what she'd expected him to say. He was basically shutting down all possibility of them being together in any way other than as business associates.

Though, maybe she should have expected him to hold himself to a high moral standard. There was that cowboy code and all that.

Most surprising was Bonner's ability to read her. She'd been caught daydreaming, imagining him and her together under her Maverick Western red and black buffalo plaid cashmere sofa throw.

This cowboy had not only noticed, but had interpreted her thoughts correctly. It was all very intriguing. His speech may be slow, but his mind was quick as a whip and he sure as hell had her pegged.

Her cheeks heated with the combination of shame and desire. She wasn't backing down though. She didn't get where she was in life by giving up easily. "So let me make sure I have this straight. You're assuming I'm interested in you *and* you're turning me down, all in the same sentence?"

"Yes, ma'am."

Huh. Somehow that only made her want him more.

She really needed to see a therapist about her addiction to challenges, and cowboys for that matter, but right now she had a man to put in his place.

Casey Harrington didn't give up on anything she wanted. Not in her career, and not with men. Bonner had no hope of sticking to his code now that Casey was determined to have him.

She tilted her head to one side. "I can assure you, Mr. Boyd—"

"You can call me Bonner."

"Can I call you Blue?" She already knew the answer but enjoyed his reaction as he frowned.

"No."

Relishing in the game, Casey smiled and took one step forward. She had to give him credit, he didn't back up, though he looked like he was torn between standing his ground and running for the hills.

"Okay, Bonner, I can assure you of two things. One, I'm

the consummate professional when it comes to my career and two..."

Casey paused for effect. It worked. She watched as Bonner swallowed and gazed down at her from much closer than he wanted to be, she was sure.

"And two?" His voice sounded husky.

She was getting to him. That made her soar with a feeling of power. "And two, were you and I ever to get together it wouldn't break any corporate or personal rules, in my opinion, but there is a very good chance we could break something else."

His Adam's apple bobbed as he swallowed. "Like what?"

Casey caught and held Bonner's gaze. "Most likely that antique bed frame in my room."

Bonner coughed and finally laughed while shaking his head. "You're not at all what I expected, Miss Casey."

"Neither are you, Bonner Boyd."

No, he was far more than she'd ever expected to find on the ranch. He was even more than she'd first assumed when he'd stepped into her headlights last night and she'd had to pry every word out of him.

She'd get this man sooner or later. Judging by the smile, she was making headway with him. But right now she decided to play it cool. She turned and followed the action as the two cowboys continued to work their asses off to get the cows into and out of the chute for the vet.

"So, you call Mr. Maverick the old man, do you?" She shot Bonner a look over her shoulder.

He let out a short laugh. "Not to his face."

"Wise decision." Casey smiled.

"So you ready to try one for yourself?" He cocked his head toward the cow checking operation before them.

Casey didn't know if he was asking her to help shove them into the tight little railed enclosure, or pull on a glove and anally probe them. Not that it mattered. Both tasks were equally unpleasant and she didn't know how to do either.

"Sure." She mustered her courage and turned to face

Bonner as he laughed and shook his head. "What, you weren't serious? Was that just a test? Do I pass?"

"Yeah, you pass." He grinned.

"Don't let me stop you from doing your job though. If you need to slap on a glove and some lube, go for it. I'll be fine here alone." She waited for his reaction.

"Wouldn't be the first time, Miss Casey. Believe me, I've checked the herd myself in past. The vet's just a whole lot faster and usually a bit more accurate than I am." He smirked.

Casey immediately got naughty thoughts regarding Bonner and the industrial-sized tube of lubricant she'd seen the vet with. She glanced sideways and found him watching her. "You know, if you've got any other *tests* for me, I'm up for just about anything."

Bonner leaned close. "Don't tease, Miss Casey." His voice was low and deadly serious.

Again he seemed to be able to read her, and all her naughty thoughts.

Interesting. Bonner Blue may live by the cowboy code, but he sure wasn't innocent.

"There's something you should know about me, Bonner." Her eyes narrowed. "I never tease."

He dropped his chin to his chest as he closed his eyes and stayed silent.

"Something wrong?"

He opened his eyes. "Yup."

"Feel like elaborating?"

Bonner stared right at her. "I'm thinking it might be best if I just give in, had sex with you and got it over with. Then maybe both of us will have some hope of getting to any work or sleep over the next week."

Once she recovered from the shock of hearing the last thing she'd ever expected to come out of Bonner's mouth, Casey smiled. She laid a hand on the front of his shirt. "Well if you're serious, make sure to grab that lube the vet's using. You can demonstrate your examination techniques for me."

His chest rose and fell beneath her touch as his breathing

quickened.

"Blue!"

"Yeah." His gaze didn't leave hers even as he answered Dakota.

"There's a whole bunch of 'em open. I've never seen this many not bred in one year. What do ya want us to do? Are we supposed to cull them all? Or do you want to save some for breeding next year?"

He drew in a deep breath. Still looking a bit dazed from her suggestion, Bonner hooked a thumb in Dakota's direction. "I gotta—"

"I understand. I'll be here when you get back."

Bonner turned on his heel and she heard him mumble, "That's what I'm worried about."

Casey smiled.

Yup. The best way to absorb the cowboy lifestyle was to just jump right into it…or on top of one.

CHAPTER SIX

"You heading up to look for stragglers?" The old man glanced at Bonner over the rim of his coffee mug.

"Yup." Bonner had gotten another shitty night's sleep. He'd finally given up and come to the main house early.

The coffee was ready even if breakfast would be awhile. And it meant he could sit in peace for a bit before Justus, Dakota, and the distraction that was Miss Sex-in-Boots herself came in.

"You taking Miss Casey with you?"

Bonner glanced at the old man. "I wasn't planning on it."

Not that he liked the idea of leaving her alone all day on the ranch with Dakota and Justus, but he liked it a hell of a lot better than being alone with her up at the summer pasture.

"Why not?" Jake took a swig and cringed, putting what must be his doctor-prescribed decaf down on the table.

"Well first off, I'm betting she can't ride."

"So teach her."

Bonner stared at Jake, eyes wide. "Teach her? Just like that?"

"Sure. Why not?" Jake shrugged. "I watched you give my grandson a riding lesson when you were just a youngin' not

45

much older than him yourself."

"Riding in a ring on a pony is one thing. Riding up to the summer pasture to find the stragglers and drive them down is another."

"She wants to learn about ranch life. This is part of cattle ranching. I want her to see it all. It's important."

"Important for her job as Maverick Western's marketing director? Or important to you because you know I don't want to do it and you enjoy messing with me?" Bonner waited.

"Both, but the second one you mentioned gives me the most enjoyment. Unlike this crud." He pushed his coffee mug away with a scowl and began eyeing the mug in Bonner's hand.

"Oh, no. Stay away from my coffee." Bonner pulled the mug closer to him, then an idea hit. "Although, perhaps a trade is in order."

"What ya got in mind?" The old man lifted a brow.

"I give you my coffee, you let me head up to get the stragglers alone." Bonner kept his voice low so Mrs. Jones didn't catch them both. Then there'd surely be hell to pay.

Sacrificing his caffeine was well worth it if it meant he wouldn't have the temptation that was Casey Harrington right there next to him all day.

Him, alone with her and the memory of the very suggestive comments she'd made yesterday—that had trouble written all over it.

"Nope. No deal." With his lips in a tight line, the old man shook his head.

"How about I agree to hook you up with my coffee every day this week." Bonner watched the old man shake his head again. "Next week too?"

Jake frowned. "Why wouldn't you want to spend the day with a woman like her? Craziest thing I ever heard. You young guys don't know which end's up half the time."

"That's not the problem." Bonner knew which end was what. *That* was the problem—Miss Casey's very fine rear end.

"Nope, you can keep your offer. I'm willing to sacrifice

myself for the good of the company and to torture you. Besides, I'll just get one of the kids to give me their coffee."

He knew Justus and Dakota would give in and do it, too. Bonner sighed. "All right. I'll take her. It's going to take twice as long with her along though."

"Then you better pack provisions in case you can't make it back before nightfall."

Frustrated, in more ways than one, Bonner let out a huff. "Fine."

Overnight in the cabin alone with her. Bonner twitched just at the thought. The old man really was trying to torture him. He had no idea exactly how much.

He'd have to teach her to ride, and push them both hard to make sure they got there and back before dark. If they didn't—well, a man could only fight a woman as strong willed and as tempting as Casey Harrington for so long.

Oh, yeah. Riding with Casey up to the summer pasture was going to be a problem. The minute Jake had suggested it, or rather forced the idea on him, Bonner knew it would be a bad idea.

An hour later that was proven as she stood looking at the horse he'd saddled for her as if it was a fire-breathing dragon.

"It's really high."

His brow rose. "Actually, he's on the small side. That's why I picked him for you."

"There's nothing smaller?"

"Just that pony I bought for the old man's great-grandkid."

"That sounds perfect. Can I ride her?"

"Uh, no. You're too big."

"Thanks." Casey scowled up at him.

Bonner shook his head. "I meant your feet would drag the ground and the pony's not cut out for this kind of ride anyway. Just get on. You'll be fine once you're in the saddle. You'll love it."

Still looking doubtful, Casey reached up to grab the saddle horn, raised one booted foot toward the stirrup, then put it down on the ground again. "Can't I ride with you on your horse?"

Having Casey pressed against him the whole ride to the summer pasture might just kill him. It would certainly kill his resolve. This hands-off policy was hard enough to stick to already.

With the dark denim of her jeans making her ass look exceptional and the looming possibility of an entire night alone in a one-room cabin with her he wasn't so sure of his resolve.

"There's no way I can get you to try it? For a little while? I'll walk you around in a circle. Right here. Then after you see how easy it is, we'll leave."

"You'll hold the reins and stay right here next to me the whole time I'm on there?"

"I swear." Bonner went so far as to make a crossing motion over his heart.

She pursed her lips and considered his offer for so long, he thought it was a lost cause. Finally, she said, "Okay."

"Good girl." Bonner stepped up behind her. He wrapped his hands around her and realized how narrow her waist was before it flared out to her hips.

Classic hourglass figure.

Damn. He was a sucker for that on a woman.

He cleared this throat. "Reach up. Grab the saddle horn. Foot in the stirrup. Up you go."

She succeeded in making it into the saddle and he succeeded in getting an eyeful of her heart-shaped ass as he boosted her up.

He led her for a full lap around the barn at a walk. Though if she refused to do anything more than walk at this snail's pace, the trip to the summer pasture would be pretty damn long. And the night spent at the cabin up there, even longer.

He glanced over his shoulder at her, still keeping them moving in a slow circle. "You know, I could tell the old man I decided to head up myself and told you to stay home."

"No. He'll fire me if I can't do this."

Bonner saw her tense, the fear and doubt clouding her features. It was a real concern for her. Why, he didn't know. The old man wasn't like that. But then again, he knew Jake Maverick, she didn't. "He's not going to fire you because you can't ride."

"He might. You said it yourself. Ranch people learn to ride before they can walk. I'm supposed to learn to be a ranch person."

"You can't learn a lifetime of skills in a week." He squinted up at her and noticed how the sun brought out the reddish highlights in her hair. Bonner dragged his gaze away.

"Well I'm going to have to."

"Then you're going to have to take the reins yourself, because I can't lead you by foot all the way to where we're going." He paused and waited. He was being tough on her, he knew that, but coddling wouldn't teach her to ride.

"Okay." Her voice sounded so small.

It was cute, how she was trying to be brave. He almost smiled but stopped himself.

"Now hold the reins like I showed you before." He thought he saw her hands shaking as she gripped the reins while trying to hold the saddle horn at the same time. "There's nothing to be scared of. I'm right here."

"You're not right here. You're way down there and I'm all the way up here on top of a living animal with a mind of his own." Her voice sounded a little too high pitched.

Horses could sense fear in a rider, but to say that would only make her more nervous.

Bonner was about to tell her she was the boss and she needed to let the horse know that when he saw her thigh muscle flex.

"Don't squeeze—" He tried to stop her, but Bonner couldn't get the words out fast enough. It was too late.

Casey, probably in her fear, clamped down hard on the horse with her legs, her boot heels pressing into his sides. The move sent him into a gallop.

The dog, who had been sitting quiet and watching, was

always up for a good chase. Misty took off after them, barking and making the situation worse.

Shit.

"Ease up on your legs!" Bonner shouted it as he swung into his saddle and spurred his horse into action. He caught up with the runaway, thankful Casey had somehow managed to stay on. "Misty, heel! Thunder, ho. Ho."

Bonner reached over and grabbed her reins, forcing Thunder closer to his mount. When he slowed his horse, Thunder with Casey on board, had no choice but to match their pace.

He slowed both down, coming to an eventual stop.

Still on his horse with Thunder's reins gripped tightly in his hand, Bonner pulled Casey from the saddle with one arm and set her on the ground. Once she was standing on her own two feet, he released his hold on her and then swung down.

He expected tears, hysterics even. What he didn't expect was her to look up at him with eyes bright and wild with excitement. "Oh my God. Did you see me? He was going so fast but I stayed on."

"I saw. You did great." Bonner held her by each shoulder. She was trembling like a leaf. "You okay?"

"Yes, but I'm not getting back up there again. No way."

He couldn't blame her. It was his fault. He'd put a city girl in a saddle and neglected to tell her Western horses were trained to respond to leg commands. An oversight which could have gotten her hurt. "All right. You don't have to. I'll go alone."

"No. I want to go."

"It's okay. I'll tell Jake I gave you a riding lesson this morning, and you even galloped on your own, then I went up to the summer pasture alone. You won't get fired."

"But I want to see the summer pasture. I *need* to see it." When she looked at him with those eyes, so sincere and pleading, she had power over him he couldn't explain.

Still feeling guilty for his failure as a teacher, Bonner drew in a deep breath. "All right. You can ride with me."

"On your horse?"

"Yes, on my horse." Though he knew he was going to regret it. "But we're bringing your horse with us. Maybe you'll feel confident enough to ride later and it'll be easier for me in case I have to go after any stragglers on the way down."

"Okay."

"You ready to leave?"

She nodded, though she looked less than enthusiastic about getting back on a horse again so soon.

"All right. Let's go." As he stepped up closer behind her and put his hands around her waist again, he was less than happy of her getting back in the saddle so soon, especially knowing he'd be joining her there. "And this time, don't squeeze with your legs and do not kick your heels into his sides, or he'll think you want to gallop. Actually, hold on. I'll get up first."

Bonner swung into the saddle and reached down one arm to her. "Grab my hand and swing up behind me."

She eyed the dog. "Will she stay or is she going to chase the horse?"

"She only ran after him because he was already running, but yeah, she'll stay." Bonner sent Misty a look. "Misty. Heel."

Tail wagging, Misty did as told and sat, ears forward, waiting for her next command. One female taken care of, one more to go. It was time to get Casey seated on his horse, God help him.

He hoisted her up and all too soon he felt the soft flesh of her breasts pressed against his back. "Okay? Ready?"

She had her arms wrapped around his waist like a vise. "No. I'm not in the saddle. I feel like I'm going to fall off."

With a sigh, he inched forward. "Can you fit now?"

"No."

He couldn't ride with the horn jammed into his crotch so she could fit in the saddle behind him. But he also wasn't thrilled with the alternative. Bonner drew in a breath. "Okay.

Hop down again. You'll have to ride in front of me."

It took some jostling, but finally he got her settled securely in the saddle in front of him, and then realized exactly how intimate a position they were in. His body noticed too and reacted.

With the reins of Casey's rider-less horse looped over his saddle horn and his arm around Casey as he held his own horse's reins, he tried to ignore the hardening in his jeans as they headed out on the path for the summer pasture, Misty at their heels.

"You know, this ride would probably be easier on you if we got down and dealt with what's poking me in the backside before we leave."

They weren't even off the Maverick's deeded land yet and she was already torturing him—sexually and verbally. But there was no denying it and no hiding it. Not with her backside nestled against the issue in question.

His face burnt with shame. "Probably. And for your information, the polite thing for you to do would have been to ignore it."

"Oh really? There are rules of etiquette for this kind of situation?" Her cockiness back, she shot a devilish look at him over her shoulder. "Good to know. So, have you thought any more about our conversation yesterday?"

"Nope." He probably should have just denied knowing what she was talking about but there was no question in his mind of which discussion she meant.

His saying they should just have sex and get it over with was very vivid in his mind and proof what overwhelming frustration could make a man say.

"Liar."

He drew in a deep breath. "All right, I have thought about what we talked about and it's not going to happen, so you can put it right out of your pretty little head."

Bonner spurred the horse and increased their pace a bit. The already long trip to the summer pasture was going to seem even longer thanks to this conversation.

Casey glanced back at him again. "Why not?"

"Because the old man is like a grandfather to me and it would betray his trust if I was anything but professional with you."

Though being professional was getting harder and harder—just like a certain body part. He could swear she was trying to bounce against him just to tease him.

"So because of business you won't sleep with me?" Her opinion of that was evident in her tone.

"That's right." This was the strangest conversation he'd ever had with a woman. It sure didn't help that her ass was pressed against his crotch during it while he desperately tried to talk down his hard-on.

"Humph. Stupid cowboy code."

The words cowboy code coming out of this city girl's mouth had him smiling. But still, she was bolder than a woman should be. One day, when she wasn't with someone like him who stuck to a code, it could get her into trouble.

"Aren't you at all afraid of me, Miss Casey?"

"No. Why should I be?"

"You're alone on thousands of acres of open land with a man who's basically a stranger to you. No one is nearby to help. There's no cell phone signal, as you're so fond of reminding me—"

"And you're a trusted employee of my boss who's a man well known and respected in the business world. You said yourself you're like family to him. Why wouldn't I trust you?"

"I just think it's dangerous for you to throw yourself physically at men you don't know."

She stiffened, her entire body suddenly ramrod straight and tense. "Believe it or not, I generally don't throw myself at any men at all, whether I know them or not. In fact, you were a first for me."

As bold as she was, that surprised him. "Really? Why?"

"You were different. I liked you."

He didn't miss how she'd phrased her feelings about him in the past tense. He should be happy. This was what he wanted. No more temptation to break his own rule. If she was pissed at him, there was no worry they'd be having sex. Perfect.

But damn, it had been nice to daydream.

It was crazy. He hadn't wanted it to happen, but now that there was no hope, he was disappointed.

Casey let out a huff of air. "Let's just get these stupid cows. Though you're probably only going to cull them—which I asked Justus about, by the way. Lovely euphemism for slaughtering them just because they're not pregnant. As if it's their fault. Probably the bull's fault. Bet you never think of that, do you?"

"Casey—"

"Do you cull the bulls too? Or just the poor old barren cows?"

This was quite a rant he'd sent her into. "Casey."

Her entire posture changed again. "What?"

"It was inconsiderate of me to say that to you. I'm sorry. I was wrong."

She remained very still in front of him "It's okay."

Bonner prided himself on being good at reading both people and animals and something had shifted within Casey. "No, something's wrong. Talk to me."

"I accept your apology. I'm fine. You just surprised me." Her voice was softer than before. Less cocky.

"Surprised you how?"

"You called me Casey instead of Miss Casey."

He considered that. "Yeah, I guess I did. That upset you?"

"No." She surprised him by laughing. "Not at all. I liked it."

Bonner let out a short laugh of his own. "Are all New York women as hard to figure out as you?"

"Only the ones who are worth it." Casey glanced over her shoulder with a smirk. Her complete turn around in mood—yet again—surprised him.

Flirty Casey was back and oh man, was he in trouble.

CHAPTER SEVEN

The cadence of the horse's movements, combined with the heat of Bonner's body pressed behind her, cradling her, probably could have rocked Casey to sleep.

The main reason she didn't drift off was Bonner and the need he created inside her with the ever present feel of his arm wrapped around her. She knew it was to keep her secure in the saddle, but his large, warm hand pressed against her stomach made her imagine all sorts of things.

She'd wished at least a hundred times he'd move his hold a few inches lower.

The thought of him sliding down and using those long fingers of his to stroke her where she so desperately craved to be touched had her undone. It would have been a lovely, peaceful ride if she weren't ready to rip off both their clothes and take care of the ache that only seemed to grow with every passing mile.

It seemed as if they'd been in the saddle for hours. The sun was high above them so perhaps they had ridden straight through the morning and into the afternoon. Casey didn't wear a watch and Bonner hadn't let her bring her cell or her tablet, saying there'd be no signal where they were going and checking for it would only upset her.

He was probably right. After the panic of being without any technology had passed, she found it was kind of freeing.

Without the distraction of texts or emails or taking notes, she took the time to look around her. It was a nice change to live in the here and now. In fact, here and now would be the perfect time and place to pull over, park this horse and roll around on one of the blankets she saw rolled and strapped behind both saddles.

The length of the trip hadn't done anything to diminish her desire to have this man. It had only increased it, tenfold. She should try and take her mind off him and that tempting bulge of his pressing into her before she lost her mind and attacked him.

Not usually one to do what she should do, Casey leaned back a little farther against him. He tightened his hold around her ever so slightly and her insides turned molten.

"It's so beautiful here." Her voice came out sounding huskier than usual. Damn, if just this cowboy's arm around her could give her sex voice, she could only imagine what having all of him all over her could do.

"Yup."

His deep voice coming from so closely behind her sent a shiver through her body. She wanted to hear him again. Feel the warmth of his breath brush her ear. Feel the tenor of his response vibrate through her as she pressed against him.

"I wish I had a camera with me. I'd love to capture all this to bring back to New York."

He shook his head. They were so close together she felt him do it. "It's best to see it with your eyes, not from behind a lens. Memory is the best camera."

Between the combination of their physical proximity, his rich, sexy voice and the fact he'd proven time and again that he could read her like an open book, she was a total goner for this guy.

Add in that he was the epitome of her ideal of a perfect man, a real life version of the Cowboy Cody she'd fallen in love with as a child, and she had no hope.

Casey loved the whole idea of him, and if she didn't watch out, she'd be in love with the man himself by the time she left for New York.

Hell, she was already in lust with him. Her stomach and parts lower had been in a permanent clench since yesterday. And now he was delivering what amounted to cowboy poetry, all while his hand warmed her belly and his length rubbed against her ass.

She turned her head enough to see his face so close behind her. "Wow. That was…beautifully spoken."

He smiled. "You're wishing you could write it down for your notes, aren't you?"

No, I'm wishing you'd kiss me.

Casey cleared her throat. "You're right."

His chuckle vibrated through her back.

"So how long until we're there?"

"Not long now. You getting tired?" He shifted in the saddle until his face was so close to hers, his chin rested against her hair.

"No. I'm fine." Definitely not too tired for what she had in mind. Casey swallowed hard. "Are we spending the night up there?"

Please, please, please…

There was a pause that seemed to stretch on forever as the pull between them became almost palpable. "Depends."

"On what?"

"How quick I can round up the stragglers. If you can ride back on your own horse so I can keep them together and moving on the trail." His voice sounded huskier, lower, closer…

It wasn't her imagination that they were pressed as tightly together as two people could be without actually having sex. His hold around her was unyielding, which was perfectly fine with her.

"I think I could ride back on my own," she turned her head toward him, "tomorrow."

They'd slowed to nearly a crawl, the reins slack in Bonner's left hand as he held her with his right. The two horses seemed to know where to go on their own.

His horse Morgan plodded with Thunder trailing along without much direction from Bonner, which was good, since he wasn't watching the path at all. Instead, he was staring directly at her. She held the eye contact as her breath became shallow.

Kiss me. She hoped he'd hear the silent plea she sent. He was so close. Just the slightest movement would put him right where she wanted him.

Bonner's chest rose and fell behind her. "Casey, if we spend the night in that cabin... I don't know what will happen."

"That's fine."

"I don't do things half way."

"Good. I don't want half way. I wouldn't mind two or three times all the way though."

She felt him shift behind her. He moved an inch closer and then his mouth was on hers, kissing her, hard and demanding. Nothing gentle about it.

His kiss was as intense as the man himself. He wrapped his arm farther around her waist, spreading his fingers wide as if trying to touch more.

More was good. She craved his bare skin against hers and sighed against his mouth.

As the horses came to a stand still, Casey tipped her head back and Bonner took the kiss deeper. He plunged his tongue between her lips and she gladly accepted, opening to him.

When he broke away, he let out a long huff of a breath. "If we pick up the pace we can be at the cabin in a few minutes. You think you can hang on?"

"Will you keep holding on to me?"

He laughed, but his heavily lidded gaze held no humor. "Darlin', keeping my hands on you is not a problem."

"Okay. Let's go." After that darlin', delivered in a voice hot enough to melt her, he could put her on a race horse in the Kentucky Derby and she'd be okay with it, if the finish line were a bed in a cabin with Bonner in it.

"Good." He looked as if he was as relieved as she was that the torture would be over soon and they'd get to what had been coming for days now.

He made a clicking sound and seemed to barely make a move, yet somehow they went from a complete stand still, to speeding down the trail. The wind whipped her hair back from her face as they sped ahead, the horses' hooves pounding against the dirt, eating up the distance between them and their destination.

It was scary and exhilarating at the same time.

Bonner on horseback galloping across the countryside seemed so natural, as if he was born to be here. Then again, he had been born and bred to this life, and for now she got to share it with him. That sent a thrill through her she'd never experienced with any other man.

The outline of a few buildings clustered together on a hilltop came into view. Her heart rate sped faster. As they neared, she could make out the cabin and some sort of three-sided shed with a fence around it. She felt him lean forward just a bit. The horse seemed to pick up speed in response to its rider's cue, or maybe Thunder just sensed the excitement in both riders.

They maintained the speed until they were nearly upon the cabin, then Bonner pulled up on the reins. They halted directly in front of the door.

He swung down to the ground and reached up for her. "I have to take care of the horses."

Casey saw the need in his eyes. It mirrored her own. With her mouth feeling dry, she swallowed. "Hurry back."

"Believe me. I will." He encompassed her waist with both hands. One moment she was in the saddle, and the next she was standing on wobbly legs between the horse and Bonner.

He kept hold of her, which was good since after so long on top of the horse she wasn't feeling very steady. Not to mention that she just plain liked his hands on her. He bent low and dropped a quick, hard kiss on her mouth and then released her. As she remained rooted to the spot, unable to take either her eyes or her mind off him, he grabbed hold of both horses' reins and led them toward the fenced area.

Misty went with her master.

Quicker than Casey ever could have, he had the horses stripped of their tack. They wandered off to seek grass to chew on as Bonner latched the gate shut, then jogged back to her, their bags in one hand and the two rolled blankets under his arm.

Unlike the mating dance that happened at the end of her usual dates in the city, where both she and her date tried to judge if there'd be a goodnight kiss, or an invitation inside for a drink or more, she didn't have to worry about any awkwardness. They both knew what was coming.

Bonner stopped only long enough to grab one more kiss before he grinned and reached for the doorknob. "Come on in."

The dog followed them up onto the small porch. "What about Misty?"

"She can stay outside. Close the door."

"Sorry, Misty," she mouthed as the dog sat, wagging her tail hopefully. Casey felt bad, but she stepped into the dim interior of the cabin, turned and shut the door in the poor dog's face.

One quick glance and she could take in the contents of the single room—a plain wooden table and a few chairs, a wood burning stove with a stack of split firewood nearby, and most importantly, beds. Two to be exact, but she was more than sure they'd only need one.

Bonner dropped the bags onto the unfinished floorboards and strode to one of the beds. As he unrolled one of the blankets, he glanced back at her. "I'll make a fire. Later."

He whipped the blanket out. It had barely drifted down and settled on the mattress before he was in front of her again. Then she was no longer standing as he lifted her off her feet and, kissing her for the duration of the short trip across the small room, carried her to the bed.

She landed on the mattress with a bounce, and looked up to see him undoing his belt buckle.

When this man made up his mind to do something, even something he'd claimed he'd been opposed to doing originally, he didn't waste any time. She watched, breathless, as he tossed his hat onto a peg sticking out of the wall and went on to pull the blue shirt from where it had been tucked into his jeans.

He made short work of the snaps and then she was faced with her first view of what real work—the outdoor, physical kind—did to a man's body.

Bonner was all hard muscle and sharp lines, his shoulders broad and his waist narrow, his stomach punctuated with washboard abs. A barbed wire tattoo wrapped around one bulging bicep, while a small cross with words and what looked like a date she couldn't make out from where she lay marked the opposite shoulder.

Shirtless, he sat on the edge of the other bed and reached to pull off one of his boots. He glanced at her. "You waiting for me to undress you?"

"Maybe." The racing of her pulse made even that one word hard to get out.

One boot hit the floor with a clunk, followed by the other. He stood again to unbutton his jeans.

"You city girls. Whole lot a' work, if you ask me." He shook his head and grinned.

"But we're worth it."

"Something I'm sure I'm about to find out for myself." His grin grew broader. In nothing but boxer briefs and socks, Bonner strode to the bed and reached for her foot. He pulled her boot off and dropped it to the floor next to his. "I'm warning you, darlin'. I've been ready to shoot off the whole ride here. I can't promise this first time is going to last very long."

He yanked the second boot off her foot, dropped it and reached down toward the button at her waist.

"That's fine. You can make it up to me the second time."

Groaning, he unfastened her jeans and pulled them roughly down her legs. She felt like a heroine in a romance novel, being taken by the hero. Carried away. Stripped. Ravished.

After being in charge of everything for so long—her department at work, her single life at home—it was nice that Bonner took complete control.

As her jeans hit the floor next to his, his gaze settled on the lace of her panties. She didn't miss the appreciation in his eyes as he perused the half of her exposed to his view and to the chill of the air.

Goosebumps rose on the skin of her legs and a shiver ran through her in spite of how hot Bonner had her on the inside.

"You're cold." He reached for the other blanket, unrolled it and covered her. Lifting one corner, he crawled into the bed with her and then Bonner's mouth covered hers again.

He settled his legs in between hers and pulled the blanket higher over them both, but with the heat of Bonner's skin covering her, she didn't think she'd need it.

Besides that, he'd left her sweater on, probably because he'd seen her chills. Rough and tough on the outside and a big softy on the inside, this cowboy never stopped amazing her.

Bonner snaked his hand between them and slipped beneath the edge of her panties.

Her breath caught in her throat as he pressed directly on her G-spot with his fingers while putting pressure on her sensitive bundle of nerves with his thumb.

It was like he knew exactly where she'd been imagining, craving, needing his touch the entire ride. He moved to bite her ear while his hand worked her faster and Casey gasped.

She tilted her hips, seeking more. He gave it to her.

At his increased pressure, she felt the orgasm build.

Her muscles clenched around his finger inside her, and her breath came faster. She was so close. Casey bit her lip but she couldn't control the sounds of pleasure, which grew louder.

Bonner lifted his head and gazed down at her. "No one can hear us way out here."

He dipped his head lower again and ran his teeth over the skin of her throat.

His fingers worked her harder and that was all it took to send her over the edge. She shattered inside. With her hips bucking against his hand, she came loud and hard.

Her body still throbbed with aftershocks when he asked, "You warm yet?"

"Yes." She nodded.

"Good." In one swift motion, Bonner whipped Casey's sweater off over her head.

He pushed the lace of her bra aside and latched onto her nipple. He sucked hard, and then scraped the tender flesh with his teeth. Her eyes drifted closed as she arched her back and pressed into his mouth. His every touch turned her inside out.

Bonner didn't give her a second to recover from the first orgasm, before rising up on his knees and pulling both of their underwear off.

She got to see and admire what she'd felt jabbing into her all day, right before he lifted her knees and sunk inside her. He closed his eyes and groaned as he pushed deep. Still sensitive from coming, the feel of him sliding in made Casey drag in a hard, shuddering breath.

When his length filled her completely, she found herself wrapped in his arms, his weight pressing her into the mattress as he drove into her. Casey had thought her vibrator a good substitute for sex, but there was no replacement for this—his mouth all over her face and neck, his soft groans in her ear, his big rough hand beneath her ass raising her to meet his every thrust, the heat of his body, the smell of his skin.

In moments she was grasping his incredible butt and holding him deeper as she worked toward another climax. "Yes. Keep going. Just like that. Oh, God."

The orgasm gripped her. Her spasms rhythmically gripped

him with a powerful orgasm that had her crying out.

His breathing grew rapid and loud, his strokes fast and hard, matching the convulsing grip of her muscles surrounding him. He stiffened over her.

"Casey." He gasped. "Do I need to pull out or can I come inside you?"

"I'm on the pill." For the first time in a very long time, Casey was very happy about that fact.

Bonner thrust hard a few more times and then came with a shout. He collapsed over her, his body heaving as he fought to catch his breath.

Casey ran her fingers over the tattoo on his shoulder. It read *John Boyd, Father*, and the date listed was nearly ten years ago. She didn't ask about it but somehow she felt as if she knew so much more about Bonner after seeing it.

She wanted him to know something about her too.

"Bonner. I'm on the pill because I was having some problems, physically, and the doctor thought it might help. It's not because...of any other reason."

No boyfriend. No fuck-buddy even. Just little old her. Available. Make that *very* available.

He lifted his head like it was an effort and dropped a kiss on her lips. "Whatever the reason, I'm very glad."

Bonner pulled out and rolled off her. Naked except for the grey socks with red cuffs he still wore, he walked to where he'd dropped the bags when they'd first come in. Even the socks didn't diminish the beauty of him, from the adorable dimples in his white ass, to the dusting of dark hair that led down from his flat belly to the tempting length between his legs.

Bonner bent over and reached into his bag to take out a small towel. He came back to her and pressed it between her legs, holding it there for a moment before wiping her clean. No man had ever bothered to do that for her before. It was all a little bit awkward, but actually, kind of sweet of him.

"I should have carried water back from the pond and heated it on the woodstove before we did anything. That way you'd have warm water to wash up."

"There was no way we could have waited for you to do all that." Casey shook her head.

He smiled. "You're probably right about that."

Standing, he balled up the towel and tossed it at his bag. When he turned back toward her, his smile had disappeared. He drew in a long breath, letting it out slowly as he bent and pulled on his boxer briefs.

Casey frowned at the sudden change in his demeanor. "What's wrong?"

Squatting by the stove, he shoved some paper and twigs inside. He met her gaze only briefly, before avoiding it again to focus on lighting a match. "I did exactly what I promised myself we wouldn't do."

"Bonner, it's okay."

He shook his head and swung the door of the stove shut as the paper inside caught fire. "It's like I let the old man down."

"He'll never know. And even if he were to find out, we're both single consenting adults. We didn't do anything wrong."

"Well yeah, according to the pastor at church we did, but I wasn't no virgin before this so that's not what's bothering me the most." His gaze found hers. "It doesn't matter if the old man knows or not. I know."

She braced herself on one elbow. "You're not exactly making me feel real good about this right now, Bonner."

"Has nothing to do with you. It's me I'm disappointed in." He opened the door and tossed two small pieces of wood into the stove. After securing the door, he came back to the bed and pulled her into his arms. "I'm sorry I made you feel bad."

Bonner kissed her with as much fervor as he did before beating himself up about what they'd done. She felt him start to grow hard again against her. When he finally pulled back, she ran her hands down his arms.

"After what you'd said, I was afraid you wouldn't want to touch me again."

"That wouldn't help any." He shrugged. "Milk's already been spilt."

She glanced down. "Yeah, it has, so to speak."

Bonner shook his head and finally laughed. "You're so clever. And bold."

"I try. Now how about we spill some more?"

"All right, but this time, it's my way." He stood and with a hand on each of her hips, flipped her over so she was facedown on the mattress.

She glanced over her shoulder at him. "What made the first time *my* way?"

"Women like it face to face. Every man knows that. It's fine with me, but this is the way I like it best." He punctuated his final word with an open-handed slap against her ass cheek.

Casey jumped. "Ow."

"Mmm, come on. That didn't really hurt." He leaned low over her back. "I bet I can make you forget all about it."

Spreading her legs a little wider, Bonner slid into Casey, forcing a sigh from her. He rocked his hips forward and drove deeper as he stroked the globes of her ass with his palms. "Beautiful."

She tried not to be insulted he'd delivered the compliment to her ass rather than her face.

It was hard to feel anything except him, stroking slowly into her as he bumped her G-spot with each stroke.

Casey sunk down lower, pressing the side of her face against the blanket while her ass poked high into the air for Bonner's taking. It changed the angle of his entry. She bore down, clenching her muscles, making the sensations shooting through her even more intense.

Bonner must have felt it to. He groaned in response. He moved his hands over her. Over the fleshy cheeks chilled from the cold air of the cabin.

"Damn, you feel good." He increased the speed of his thrusts.

Casey drew in a sharp breath at the sensation. She moaned

and pushed her butt higher.

"You like that?" he asked.

"Yes," she breathed.

Bonner pumped into her faster.

Casey lost track of time until his strokes sped to a crescendo before he drove hard and held himself deep, pulsing inside her again before he collapsed. For the second time that day, Bonner had her pinned to the bed, panting above her. She didn't mind a bit.

He rolled to his side and pulled her back against his chest. "There's no way we're heading home today." The warmth of his breath brushed her hair as he spoke, his head just above hers, his arms wrapped around her.

"Good."

"Canned chili okay for dinner? Pickings are slim here."

"That sounds perfect."

Bonner let out a snort. "You're a good liar."

Casey turned in his arms to face him. "Except for the few times a year I visit my parents or my sister, I live on gourmet take-out from some restaurant or another in the city, but never once have I ever had a hot cowboy cook me chili over a fire while I snuggle under a wool blanket, exhausted from countless orgasms. So it does sound perfect."

"Since you put it that way..."

"There is one thing." Casey hesitated. "Um, what do we do about a bathroom?"

Bonner chewed on his lip, looking like he was considering how to answer. "Well, there's the outhouse."

"Outhouse." She didn't like the sound of that.

He nodded and got up, but she didn't miss his grin.

"Go out the door and around back. It's about thirty yards behind the cabin. You can't miss it." Casey's eyebrows shot high as Bonner bent down and grabbed her boots off the floor. "We're alone up here so no need to get dressed except that you might get chilled, but you better at least put on your boots. Snakes. Oh, and don't forget this."

Bonner reached for a shelf and handed her a roll of toilet

paper.

She stood, taking the boots in one hand and the toilet paper in the other, and stared at him. "You're not kidding, are you?"

It wasn't really a question. She knew the answer, but she could have done without the man who'd just given her the best sex of her life looking so smug about the situation.

"Sorry."

Casey sighed. "Fine. But I'm wearing your shirt to go outside."

She scanned the floor and found it. Casey picked it up and read the label. "Maverick Western? One of the perks of the job?"

"The old man gave me a whole dang case of the same exact shirt for Christmas last year after I was bitching I'd torn mine on the barbed wire while fixing some fencing."

Casey sat on the edge of the mattress and tugged on her boots. "Ah, that explains a lot. I thought you just had a strange obsession with wearing blue shirts. So that's not why your nickname is Blue? I'd had a whole scenario worked out in my mind."

"No, it's not."

"If you don't tell me the reason the guys call you Blue, I'm just going to make one up, and I can assure you, it likely won't be flattering." She stood and slipped on Bonner's shirt.

"The nickname's not a big deal. I came out of my mama with the cord around my neck and my father called me his little boy blue. That's all."

She frowned at him. "That's not that big of a deal."

He shrugged one shoulder. "I never said it was."

She sighed as she buttoned the shirt, deciding she'd have to deal with his aversion to his nickname later. Now, she had to pee.

His shirt was long enough on her to make a decent dress. She retrieved the toilet paper off the bed where she'd laid it and turned to find him watching her and smiling. "What?"

Bonner grinned broader. "You look good in my shirt."

"Yeah, well, I might just keep it then." Why did that thought give her a little tingle?

Bonner shrugged again. "Go right ahead. I have more."

"Fine. I will." After that victory she realized she still had the humiliation of the outhouse to face. She strode out the door with as much dignity as a woman wearing cowboy boots and a man's shirt while carrying a roll of toilet paper could.

The dog trailing behind her adding to the surreal feel of the situation, Casey could hear Bonner chuckling until after she'd closed the door and turned the corner of the house. Then she saw her first outhouse.

Standing outside of the tall skinny building, its door still closed, Casey eyed the wooden structure. She glanced down at the dog. "Misty, you think there's spiders in there?"

The dog's pointed black and white speckled ears perked up as she sat, tail wagging. With her strange eyes, one blue and one brown, she watched Casey.

Casey briefly considered sending the dog inside first to scare away any animals. She reached out and flung the door open fast, and then jumped back in case any sort of creature rushed her. When nothing came out, she took one step forward and peeked inside.

It was pretty dark in there. She supposed she could pee with the door open so she'd have some light to see anything coming at her. She took a step in and peered at the wooden seat. There could be all sorts of bugs nesting under that thing. Maybe she'd be better off squatting behind the building than inside it.

But wait, hadn't Bonner mentioned snakes?

Casey was just deciding the best course of action, the lesser of two evils, when she heard Bonner's laugh. With each passing second she became more certain that though she'd thoroughly enjoyed the cowboy inside, having to actually live like a cowboy and use this outhouse was pure crap—no pun intended.

She turned back to face the cabin and saw him, fully dressed right down to a blue shirt that matched the one she had on. He leaned against the corner of the cabin, his hat pulled low, leather chaps strapped to each leg. She would have found those chaps incredibly sexy if he weren't laughing at her so hard he had to wipe at his eyes.

Casey crossed her arms. "This isn't funny. There could be deadly black widow spiders inside there. Or, or, worse. Like scorpions. Or copperhead snakes."

"Don't worry." Grinning, he strode toward her. "Rat Snake or a rattler maybe, but I never found a copperhead in these parts. And scorpions are nocturnal and it's still daylight, so you're fine." Bonner pushed past where she hovered in the doorway and stepped inside the small building. He lifted the wooden seat. "See. Nothing in there that shouldn't be in there."

"What about underneath? It could be hanging there waiting to bite me in the butt."

That brought on another bout of laughter, until Bonner literally had to wipe the smile off his face with one hand. He sobered enough to take each of her arms in his grasp. "Look. I'm very fond of that ass, and I wouldn't let you do anything to jeopardize it. Okay?"

She glanced at the hole again, then back at him, not convinced.

"Okay, how about this." Bonner glanced around them and then picked up a stick. He used it to bang hard on the wooden seat. Nothing came running up at him. Then he sat, still fully clothed, on the seat himself. He stood and turned his backside to face her. "Any deadly critters hanging off my ass?"

"No."

"All right then. Your turn."

"You had your jeans on."

He physically steered her into the building. "I'll be right here waiting for you."

She wasn't sure she was onboard with that idea. She'd wanted that door to stay open so she could see and make a quick escape if necessary, but not with Bonner standing right there. Sure they'd had sex, twice, but peeing in front of a man was something you didn't do until you were dating for a really long time, or living together, or married. Or maybe drunk.

He sighed. "What's wrong now?"

"Turn your back…and cover your ears."

His brows rose high. "Should I sing la-la-la too?"

"Please, just do it. This is stressful enough."

"All right." Shaking his head at her, he turned and covered his ears. "Go on. Get to it."

Talk about pressure.

Finally, she got done what she'd needed to do, and though she'd lived through the peeing, she couldn't help but consider if she could avoid doing it again before they got back to the ranch tomorrow.

Probably not. That was a long time away.

With a sigh, she grabbed her toilet paper roll after almost forgetting where she'd hung it on the big nail sticking out of the wallboard and left the confines of the outhouse.

Out in the daylight again, she adjusted Bonner's shirt and said, "Okay. I'm done."

He nodded. "Good. Now I'm gonna have to go look for the stragglers."

"And leave me here?"

"Well, I can find them and bring them back here quicker on my own, but if you're afraid to be alone, I can take you with me."

"I'm not afraid. It's just…I don't have my cell phone."

"Yes, I know." He smiled again. "But if I go alone, I'll be able to get 'em back here within an hour. Then we can decide if you want to head home today and try to beat sunset, or stay and leave at first light tomorrow. Since you don't seem to like the facilities, I thought you might want to get back to the ranch sooner rather than later."

She glanced back at the outhouse. "Okay. Go on your own."

Bonner nodded. "I put wood in the stove so you should be okay 'til I get back."

Casey certainly hoped so. He turned toward the horses, when she took one step after him. "Bonner?"

He pivoted back. "Yeah?"

"Hurry back."

He grinned. "I will. Promise."

She watched him saddle his horse and stood in front of the cabin like some pioneer woman as he rode away. He even took the dog. She was all alone. As cut off as if she were actually living back in the pioneer days.

With a sigh, Casey turned back and went inside the cabin. The fire had made it warmer inside. It wasn't too bad. It would be better with Bonner there though.

She glanced at the bed. They'd made quite the jumble of it.

Casey straightened the bottom blanket and then folded the top one, laying it on the end of the mattress. She tried to decide what to do next to kill the time.

Missing her tablet, she was at a loss for something to do. Her gaze landed on two cans of chili Bonner must have left on the table.

What the hell. Might as well take this experience all the way. Casey found a can opener and a spoon and for the first time in years, began to cook dinner.

All right, she couldn't really call it cooking since all she did was open a can and put it in a pan on the woodstove, but she did add a log to the stove just to make sure the fire kept going, so that increased the degree of difficulty.

Cooking without benefit of electricity or gas—that was pretty impressive if she did say so herself.

She'd just stirred the chili in the cast iron skillet, much like the Maverick Western one she owned in New York except this one looked like it had actually been used, when she made out the faint sound of a dog barking.

Misty.

Casey couldn't help but smile. Bonner was back. She strode to the door and out onto the porch.

The sun's rays as it sunk lower in the sky highlighted the cloud of dust in the distance. Through it she could make out about half a dozen cows, running, while Bonner rode behind them. As they got closer, she could see Misty as she wove from side to side behind the herd of cattle, barking and nipping at their hooves.

But it was the figure on horseback, the man who occasionally swung a rope and yelled to the animals, who drew and held her attention once again.

She couldn't keep her eyes off Bonner. God, he was extra sexy when he was doing cowboy stuff.

The scene before her was like a Western movie come to life.

No, more accurately, Casey felt as if she'd stepped into an episode of the Cowboy Cody show. She was the little woman holding down the homestead waiting for her man with a hot meal and even hotter sex. While he was the man riding home after a long time away tending the herd at the summer pasture.

By the time Bonner had slowed the herd to a walk and funneled them into the fenced in area bordered on one side by a pond, she was ready to tear his clothes off and mount him on the front porch.

As he carried a bucket of water to the cabin, and she saw his smile and the color in his cheeks from the ride, that idea was sounding better and better to her.

"Welcome back." Casey heard the breathless quality in her own voice again. Bonner did that to her.

"Told you I wouldn't be long." He pushed past her and set the bucket on the floor next to the stove. He glanced back. "You started dinner. Good. I'm starving."

"Then let's eat." There was only one thing Casey wanted to eat, but she'd better feed the cowboy first. He'd need his strength for later.

Bonner grabbed two bowls and another spoon off a shelf and carried them back to the table.

With a leather glove he pulled from his belt, he took the hot pan off the stove and put it on the table. She couldn't do much more than watch as he served them both. Her stomach was so twisted with need, she wouldn't be able to eat much of the chili, but that didn't stop her from enjoying watching him.

He'd emptied his bowl before he glanced up at her. "You all right? You're not eating."

"I'm not hungry right now." At least not for what was in the bowl. Casey stood and, facing him, straddled Bonner in his chair.

He supported her with a hand on each cheek of her ass. "Not that I'm complaining, but what got into you?"

"You." She planted a hand on each side of his face and kissed him, deep and thorough.

With a groan he picked her up. She wrapped her legs around his waist as he walked them both to the bed.

He laid her on the mattress and rolled to lie on his side as he gazed down into her face. "If this is the welcome I'm going to get, maybe I'll let the stragglers loose and go round them up again tomorrow."

"Sounds good to me." She pushed him onto his back and unbuckled his belt. He smelled of leather and horse and the outdoors.

"Let me take my chaps and boots off." Bonner moved to sit up.

"Oh no. Those stay on. The spurs too."

His eyebrows shot up, but he reclined again without complaint.

It took a bit of doing, but she freed him from the fly of his jeans.

Leaving the rest of his clothes on Casey leaned low. She took his length between her lips and tasted the salty flavor of him.

Bonner groaned, low and deep in his throat. "Damn, girl. Are you living out some city girl-cowboy fantasy with me?"

Casey lifted her head. He slipped out of her mouth with a pop. "Yup. That a problem?"

"Nope." He reached out and nudged her head down gently. "Go right ahead."

She did, lowering her mouth while making sure her teeth

grazed him the whole way down. He was hard and smooth, like steel covered in satin.

Bonner hissed a sharp breath and tangled his hands in her hair.

She lifted off him again, using plenty of teeth, and glanced up. "I like rough."

"Me too." Bonner's hold on her head tightened and he thrust into her mouth. That was the last talking they did for a while.

CHAPTER EIGHT

Bonner couldn't say he'd slept, more like he dozed. He also couldn't say that he cared that he didn't get a solid night's sleep. The reason for that was lying next to him now, her chestnut hair tickling his nose as they shared a pillow in the narrow bed.

He'd dare any man to try and sleep while Casey's naked body was pressed against him all night. Warm. Soft. Tempting.

The fire was nearly dead. He should get his lazy ass out of bed and build it up again so she'd be warm when she got dressed and they ate breakfast, which he'd have to break to her would be canned hash, not all that much different from the canned chili they'd had for dinner. But he couldn't bring himself to leave the bed while she was still in it.

She'd slept fine though, and still was sleeping, judging by the slow steady breathing.

He supposed he should leave her be. That thought entered and left his head as he ran one palm over the curve of her hip. She lay on her side facing away from him. It was the perfect position for him to nestle very happily against the soft flesh of her ass.

He'd been admirably restrained all night, if you asked him. Not one of the times he'd awoken hard as a rock had he woken her to relieve it.

Now though, the sun was up and so was he. All bets were off now that it was daylight.

Running his lips over her shoulder, Bonner worked his way to her ear, where he nibbled. Meanwhile, he snaked one hand around and cupped her breast.

Shame she wore sweaters all the time. He could appreciate a nice chest even though he was primarily an ass man.

Speaking of ass… He pressed his erection a little more firmly against hers.

"Someone's awake." She sounded all warm and sleepy.

"Mm, hm. All of me."

"Yes, so I feel." Casey laughed and then stretched. "Wow. I've never slept so well."

Bonner shook his head. At least one of them had. She was doing better in the cabin than he ever expected a city girl to. "Good. I'm glad of that and I owe you a compliment."

"Compliment. For what? The blowjob?"

He laughed. "Yeah, that was good, but what I was fixin' to say was, you're doing real good being away from all your computers and cell phone." Not to mention running water, and heat, and electricity.

"Thank you. I appreciate you noticing. You uh, distracting me has helped tremendously."

"Maybe I'll hide all that stuff when we get back. When you start to get twitchy, you'll have to come find me for some more…distraction." He pressed closer.

It was mind boggling how he could want her so badly again after the number of times he'd had her yesterday.

Soon they'd be back under the watchful eyes of the other guys and the old man. Bonner wasn't sure about what they'd do then. He couldn't take her to the bunk house with the others, but he didn't want to be rolling around in her bed under the same roof as the old man either.

That would seem even more disrespectful than what they

were already doing. But here and now, they were alone and she was all his.

One small move of his hips and Bonner was nudging at her. A bit of pressure and he slid into her slick warmth. Casey let out a sigh. "Mm, this is a nice way to wake up."

Oh, hell yeah it was. He could easily do this every morning.

"Mm, hm." Bonner pushed in deeper as Casey pressed back against him. He reached around and found the spot that would drive her crazy. He circled it with the tip of one finger and felt her muscles tighten around him.

It made him crave so much more with her. That should scare him. The more frightening fact was that it didn't.

"I'm close." She was breathless and gasping but he heard her loud and clear.

Bonner groaned and drove in, and then out of her. She tilted her hips forward, pressing against his hand. He pressed deeper while working her with his hand harder.

Her body convulsed around him as she cried out. That was all it took for him to lose control. He pounded hard and fast and then held deep, coming inside her as her body gripped him.

They both lay, panting, until his body slackened and slipped out of her. He squeezed her tighter, not wanting to let go even though he knew he'd have to eventually. First to clean themselves up, then to leave here and go back to the real world.

He'd never be able to walk into this cabin again without remembering this. Her.

Bonner pressed a kiss to her hair. "Thank you."

She smiled. "You're welcome."

He laid his head against hers. "I mean it."

"I know you do. I just never had a man thank me for sex before."

"It was really good sex." He smiled too.

"Thank you. And you're welcome." Casey sighed. "I'm afraid I'm going to have to go experience that lovely outhouse again."

"Want me to come with you?"

"No, I think I'll brave it on my own this time."

He rose on one elbow and looked down at her. "I'm sorry things aren't a little nicer for you here."

She rolled onto her back to face him. "Don't. Outhouse aside, this was absolutely perfect. I wouldn't have wanted it any other way."

The sincerity in her voice made him like her all the more. His little city girl, warming canned chili over a fire, braving the outhouse, sleeping like a log in a cabin.

Trying not to think about how fast the day she'd be leaving was bearing down on them, Bonner squeezed her with one more hard hug before he released her.

Casey got out of bed and padded across the room, naked except for socks until she slipped on his blue shirt. The sight tightened something in his chest. He'd never be able to put on his own damn shirt again without thinking of her and remembering this time.

Boots on, his shirt hanging nearly to her knees, and the roll of toilet paper in her hand, she looked adorable as she shot him a smile and then disappeared through the door.

Maybe he should go buy some new shirts. Red ones.

CHAPTER NINE

Bonner sat at the table and concentrated solely on his lunch of chicken thighs swimming in barbecue sauce with a side of buttery rice, afraid if he dared glance up everyone would read in his expression exactly what he was trying to hide. That he and Casey had basically done not much more than have sex in every position imaginable the entire time they'd been alone together at the cabin.

The old man shoved his plate of grilled chicken breast and plain rice away from him and sighed. "So Bonner, how was she?"

Bonner looked up, his eyes wide. He cleared his throat. "What?"

"How did the city girl do on her first cattle drive?" The old man chuckled. "You must have rode her hard if she's too tired to even eat lunch."

Justus and Dakota both snickered as Bonner's chest tightened.

They couldn't know. Of course they didn't know.

Fighting the rising guilt, Bonner reminded himself everything said would sound perfectly innocent if he hadn't done exactly that, rode Casey hard, three times, four if he counted taking her mouth.

"She did good. Better than I expected. She finally took to Thunder, so the ride down was smoother than the one up." Bonner shrugged.

"How'd she like the outhouse?" Dakota grinned.

Bonner smiled, remembering that first time. "It was pretty interesting."

"I bet." The old man chuckled. "Thank you. I know you didn't want to take her. I appreciate that you did."

"No problem." Bonner nodded and kept his eyes focused on the chicken bones on his plate.

"You sure took your time. Left us here alone to handle things. Didn't expect you to take two damn days to round up half a dozen stragglers." Justus, hands covered in sauce as he held a chicken leg, looked unhappy.

"I wouldn't have alone, smart ass. Yesterday was the first time she'd ever been on a horse." Bonner raised a brow. "And what I see you're really telling me is that you two can't handle things without me. Guess we know who carries the weight around here now, don't we?"

Dakota shot Justus a look. "We handled it just fine. Just sucked to have you gone yesterday and half of today, and you'll be out all damn day tomorrow too."

"Tomorrow?" Bonner frowned until it hit him. "The bull riding school. I forgot all about that." He glanced at the old man. "What am I going to do with her tomorrow?"

"Bring her with you."

"No. No way. The trip to the pasture was one thing, but this is different."

The old man watched him for a bit. "All right. I'm sure she'll be happy to have a day off from ranching anyway."

"We can take her with us for the day." Justus looked up hopefully.

"Oh no, you won't. You two can finish fixing that stretch of fence we didn't get to the other day. I'll show her the computer in the office. That'll keep her busy all day." Bonner figured once Casey got some technology in her hands after all this time, she wouldn't even notice he was gone. Which was exactly what he wanted.

He didn't need all the questions that her knowing he was a rodeo champion would bring. That part of his life was in his past, and that's where he wanted it to stay.

It was crazy he'd even let himself get talked into being a coach at this one-day bull riding clinic one of the local guys was throwing at his place. He must be getting soft in his old age.

Dakota sighed. "All right."

"And if she asks where I am, just tell her I'm helping out at a neighbor's. Got it?" It wasn't a lie. Just not the whole truth. So why did he feel kind of bad about it?

"Why?" Justus frowned.

"Yeah, Blue, why you always getting mad when people bring up your rodeo days?"

"Boys. Leave him be and do as he says." That one sentence, delivered in a tone that the old man had perfected from years of bossing people, shut both of the kids up.

Bonner nodded thanks and tried not to think about how her absence at this meal, and the prospect of not seeing Casey tomorrow either, had made him feel as if a cloud had just blocked out the sun.

~ * ~

Casey had never been so happy to see a shower in her life. After not even twenty-four hours at the cabin, hot running water seemed like a luxury worthy of kings and queens.

When she came out of the shower and found a tray with a hot meal waiting on the desk in her bedroom, she'd thought she'd died and gone to heaven.

She pulled on her Maverick Western flannel lounging pants and matching brushed cotton long-sleeved T-shirt. After shoving her feet into her Maverick natural fur, rubber soled slippers she sat to devour the lunch of barbecued chicken and rice.

Her tablet was powered on and propped in front of her just in case the signal decided to work today. Even if it didn't, the moment she was done with the chicken and had washed, or possibly licked, the tasty sauce off her fingers, she'd start making notes, recording her thoughts about the past two days.

Well, maybe not *all* her thoughts. Parts of her felt deliciously sore, a physical reminder of her many incredible hours with Bonner in the cabin.

She certainly hoped he and his cowboy code didn't have any delusions that now they were back and under Jake Maverick's roof and scrutiny they wouldn't be repeating those encounters, because she had other ideas.

Determined to nail down this marketing campaign and Bonner Blue Boyd, Casey cleaned up from lunch and grabbed her tablet.

Tingly with excitement about both her work and Bonner, she crawled onto her bed and settled in to do some work— and maybe daydream about her cowboy.

If Bonner needed her for anything, he'd have to come upstairs and get her.

Mmm. She liked that idea.

She must have fallen asleep, because though she'd lain down while the afternoon sun had been streaming through the panes of her bedroom window, she awoke to the grey light of pre-dawn. She had been more exhausted than she realized if she'd slept straight through dinner and through the night.

The one good thing about life on the ranch was that everyone woke early, and hot coffee was the first order of business.

Casey could get onboard with that schedule. She glanced down at herself, considering if she really needed to get dressed just to sneak downstairs and grab herself a cup. She compromised and threw on a bra under her T-shirt in case she ran into any of the men and then she headed down the back staircase. It led directly to the kitchen where she hoped Mrs. Jones and her blessed pot of caffeine were.

Down in the kitchen she didn't find Mrs. Jones, but she

did find her boss.

Surprised, but not unpleasantly so, she said, "Mr. Maverick. Good morning."

"Please, call me Jake."

She couldn't help but warm to the old man. He was so completely down to earth, even though the name Maverick had become a household word, at least in this country.

Casey smiled. "Okay, I will. You're up early."

"I have to be if I want to grab a cup of real coffee before the caffeine Nazi forces that decaf crap on me."

Sympathizing completely with the old man, Casey laughed. She'd probably curl up in a ball and die if the doctor cut her off cold turkey from real coffee. "I won't tell."

"Good girl. Keep this up and your future at Maverick Western will be long and bright."

If only hooking Jake up with caffeine were enough to insure her success.

"Thanks. I look forward to it." She laughed. "So what does Bonner have planned for me today?"

"He's gone already. He'll be gone until nightfall, so you've got today off."

What? She didn't want the day off. Not if it meant not seeing Bonner.

"Where did he go?"

"He's helping out at one of the neighbor's places."

Neighbors? Casey hadn't seen another house, or even a gate, the entire time she'd been here. "Oh? That's nice of him."

"Yup." Jake spent a good amount of time stirring the sugar into his coffee.

"What kind of help? With culling the herd or something?" Casey's question had two goals.

First, she wanted to impress Jake that she'd picked up the ranch lingo in her short time there. But mostly, she wanted to know where Bonner was and what he was doing. And why he hadn't taken her with him.

Jake got a strange expression on his face. "Uh, not real

sure. But he did leave instructions for you for the day."

"He did?" At least Casey knew he'd been thinking of her. That made up a little bit for the fact he'd abandoned her for the day.

"Yup." He cocked his head to one side. "Follow me. I gotta get out of here anyway before the coffee police gets here."

The old man led her through the maze that was the rambling old house until they ended at a tiny room way in the back. Casey hadn't even known it existed, but when Jake flipped on the light switch, she nearly dropped her coffee at what she saw.

A big old fax machine dating back to the last century if she had to guess. A printer, just as bulky as the fax machine. A desk phone, sporting an actual cord, that she hoped was connected to a landline that didn't need cell signal to work. And, what really caught her eye, the desktop computer.

It was big and old, with a monitor that took up half the desk, but if it were wired for internet, she'd kiss it.

"Is there…" Casey swallowed, afraid to hope. "Internet?"

"Yup. High-speed, or so I'm told. It's all yours to use. Phone, fax, computer, printer. Whatever you need."

Oh, thank God. She took one step forward into the room, closer to the shrine of technology. Casey finally broke her gaze away to find Jake grinning at her.

"Blue said you'd be happy. So will this keep you occupied for the day?"

Her heart fluttered. Bonner knew her too well, and she loved it.

"Oh yeah." She smiled wide. Hot coffee, even hotter cowboy sex, good home-cooked meals, beautiful scenery, and now this, the whole world-wide-web at her disposal. Casey was beginning to be able to see herself living ranch life. She glanced up at Jake. "Thank you."

He shook his head, grinning. "I'll send a search party for you if you're not out by dinner."

That was a good possibility. She laughed. "Okay."

With a nod, Jake and his contraband coffee disappeared and Casey was alone. She sat at the desk and pushed the power button. The monitor sprang to life and her heart rate quickened.

What to do first? Work email? Personal email?

Then what Jake had said stuck out—*Blue said you'd like it.* Jake rarely slipped up and called Bonner *Blue.* His doing it today reminded her of the secrets the man seemed to keep about his past.

Decision made, Casey opened an internet browser window and typed into the search field "Bonner Blue Boyd Colorado rodeo".

Up popped a list of links a page long. Her cowboy had blazed a virtual path a mile wide and it was all here, his entire past, for her to see.

It was like Christmas morning and every link was like a gift under the tree with her name on it. And unlike when she was eight, this time she knew there'd be a cowboy inside.

Casey leaned forward and clicked on the first link.

An action shot of Bonner took her breath away. One arm held high in the air, his cowboy hat pulled low, he somehow stayed on the back of a bucking bull whose four hooves were airborne.

The articles were ten years old. God, he was just a kid then, probably about the same age as Justus and Dakota.

The titles went from *State Rodeo Champion Bonner Blue Boyd Wins* to dated the following year saying *Reigning Champion Blue Boyd Retires* with no explanation for it.

Casey leaned back and frowned. Her research—she refused to call it stalking—had yielded more questions than answers.

What had made him retire at the height of his career? More importantly, why was he so reluctant to discuss that time of his life? And finally, where the hell was he today and why wouldn't Jake tell her?

CHAPTER TEN

It had to be the worst damn pain he'd ever felt.

Seriously.

In his bull riding days, Bonner had been bucked off and stomped on and still felt better afterward than he did now after one stupid yoga class.

He limped in to the dining room looking as if he'd gone eight-seconds with a champion bull and lost. Who the hell would have thought a person could injure a hamstring from doing something called the heron pose?

His quadriceps in the opposite leg didn't feel so great either.

When did bull riders start doing yoga anyway? What happened to the old days when a man could just get on a barrel or a few practice bulls to train? And what the hell had made him think that, in his thirties, he should try yoga alongside the teens and twenty-somethings at the clinic?

Well he sure had learned his lesson. No more yoga. Ever. He'd been barely able to get his boots on. He didn't even want to think about trying to get them off again.

He'd taken so long getting to the dining room from his truck, thanks to his yoga injury, the boys and the old man were already seated.

Casey however, wasn't there. Probably still eyeball deep in the computer.

Dakota looked up from his seat at the table. "Jesus, Blue. What the hell happened to you?"

Bonner groaned. "Don't ask."

The old man raised a brow. "Well, I'm asking. What's wrong with you?"

Justus frowned in sympathy. "You get bucked off at the clinic?"

"No, I didn't get bucked off. I wasn't even on a bull." Bonner scowled and lowered himself slowly into the chair.

Dakota frowned. "So then what—"

Casey appeared in the doorway just as Dakota decided he couldn't let the conversation go. If there was one person Bonner didn't want questioning him about today, which would only lead to talk of his past rodeo career, it was her.

"I'll tell you all later." Bonner shot all three men a look that would hopefully silence them, but not before Casey's expression told him she knew she'd walked in on a conversation he didn't want her to hear.

"So how was your day, little lady?" the old man asked.

Thank God for Jake. He addressed Casey with the one subject that would most likely take the attention off Bonner. The Internet.

"Very productive. Thank you. I actually printed out some preliminary marketing plans, if you're interested in seeing them."

Jake nodded. "Sure. Can't promise I'll understand 'em, but I'll take a look."

"You're being modest." Casey shook her head and then her focus moved from the old man, to him. "So, Bonner, how was your day? You miss me tagging along with you?"

He didn't miss the undertone in her question. She was most likely pissed off because they'd had what amounted to eighteen hours of straight sex and then he'd disappeared for the day without explanation. He'd have to tell her something.

"Sure did, but we got done what needed doing so it was a good day." Once again, he shot a sideways glance at the men at the table.

If they didn't ask any questions about the bull riding clinic, he wouldn't have to avoid answering them to prevent Casey from prying into his past.

"So, uh, why didn't you tell me there was high speed Internet in the house before today?" She didn't look satisfied but thankfully she let the subject of where he'd been all day drop. Though now it seemed he was in the hot seat for not showing her the office equipment right off.

"Because Jake's accountant has been in there working most of the days since you got here." Bonner grinned. "And because I enjoy torturing you."

Casey let out a short laugh. "I'm beginning to think you do."

He glanced up to find too much interest in this conversation from the others at the table. If he didn't watch it, this exchange between him and Casey would tip them all off that there was much more between them now than there had been the last time they'd all sat at this table together.

Time to change the subject again. He turned to Dakota and Justus. "So, that fencing fixed yet?"

That was followed by a bunch of excuses and explanations from the two kids, all delivered while Casey's attention stayed a little too focused on Bonner for his liking.

When the meal was done, much too soon it seemed, he had another challenge—how was he going to walk out of there without Casey noticing him limping? Maybe if he just stayed in his seat she'd leave the room first.

Yeah, that was a plan.

"We're heading into town. There's a band at the bar." Dakota stood, followed by Justus. "You wanna come, Blue?"

"Nah, that place is too loud for me."

"Miss Casey?"

As much as Bonner didn't want Casey asking questions about his injury or his past, he also didn't want her out at a bar, possibly getting drunk, with these two. He turned to watch and wait for her answer.

"Thank you, but I think I'll hang out here for the night." She shot him a glance.

"All right. See you guys in the morning." Dakota and Justus left, but Casey didn't move. She was going to stay there with him at the table. His plan to outwait her was going to backfire.

The old man stood. "I notice no one's inviting me out. That's all right. I have plans of my own."

Bonner raised a brow. "What plans?"

Jake glanced around then leaned closer. "After Mrs. Jones goes to bed, I sneak down and raid the fridge."

He couldn't help but smile. "Don't get caught."

"I've been sneaky for too long to get caught now. G'night, you two." The old man left and then there were two— Bonner and Casey. He scrambled for a safe subject. "So, I'm glad you got what you needed to get done today."

"I did. What did you get done today?" Her brow rose as she waited.

He shrugged. "Just helping out over at another guy's place. It's done now. Tomorrow we're back to normal around here."

Casey frowned. "Why are you acting so secretive? If it's just helping out at another ranch, what's the big deal? And why didn't you take me with you?"

"It's no big deal at all. It wasn't anything. Sorry. I thought you'd appreciate at day off and some technology after the past week, is all."

"I did." She sighed. "I'm sorry. And thank you."

He nodded. "You're welcome."

They sat in awkward silence. She wasn't leaving and he couldn't without limping like a ninety-year-old man with a bum leg. This was a hell of a situation he'd gotten himself in.

Maybe honesty was the best policy, but doing what was best wasn't always easy.

They seemed to be at a stand off, Casey watching him,

him looking anywhere but at her, when Mrs. Jones came into the room. "You two still here? Good. I need help in the kitchen."

"I'll help you." Casey stood.

"No, you won't. This is a man's job." Mrs. Jones motioned for Casey to sit back down. "Bonner?"

He raised a brow. "If Casey wants to help—"

"Bonner Boyd, we don't let women do the work of a man in this house. Your mama and daddy raised you better than that."

"Yes, ma'am." He pushed back his chair and braced his hands on the table. He took one step and winced, glancing up to see if Casey had noticed.

"What'd you do to yourself now?" Mrs. Jones frowned.

"Nothing. I'm fine. What do you need done?" He took one more hobbling step and then another, resisting the urge to look back at the woman whose eyes he felt boring into his back.

Mrs. Jones shook her head. "Men."

CHAPTER ELEVEN

Casey waited, arms folded, until Bonner fixed the faucet in the kitchen for Mrs. Jones and had to hobble back through the dining room to get to the front door and his truck.

Judging by the expression on his face, he hadn't expected her to be waiting. He obviously didn't know how determined she could be when she put her mind to it.

"Quite a limp you got there."

"It's nothing."

"How'd it happen?"

"Pulled something."

Casey resisted the urge to stamp her foot like a child but it wasn't easy. "Why won't you tell me?"

Bonner drew in and blew out a long, slow breath. "There's nothing to tell."

Usually when he did things slow, especially when they were in bed, she loved it. But this was just plain frustrating.

"Bonner." She feared she might have actually stamped her foot that time.

He glanced at the kitchen door. "Let's go someplace where we can talk."

"Fine." She turned and headed for the staircase to her

room, thinking that would be a pretty good place to be once they ironed this out, given she had that nice comfy bed and all. He could make his evasiveness up to her there.

Climbing the stairs looked particularly painful for Bonner. Casey tried not to take too much satisfaction in that. She was pretty pissed he was keeping secrets and avoiding her after all they'd done together.

Still she didn't want him to be in *too* much pain. Just a little...

In her room, he glanced around and then chose to sit at the desk chair. As Casey perched on the edge of the mattress she decided she'd let him stay where he was...for now.

Bonner let out a frustrated sounding breath and glanced up at her. "One of the local ranches was running a bull riding clinic for young riders and they asked me if I'd come and help out. As a coach. I ended up pulling a muscle. I'm retired and this proves I should have stayed retired. See. Told you it was nothing."

"Why did you retire?" she asked. "I mean from what I read, you were at the top of your career when you quit."

His gaze shot to her and he didn't look happy. "From what you read?"

"Um, well it was all right there on the Internet."

Bonner's brows shot up. "That's how you spent your day? Researching me?"

"No. Just for like a minute or two." Casey crossed her arms, a sick feeling in the pit of her stomach. Why was he being so secretive? "What's wrong, Bonner. What are you hiding?"

She hoped she didn't regret asking that question as he finally looked her in the eye. "I retired because my wife wanted me to."

"Your wife?" The word nearly doubled Casey over with nausea. "This may be a little late to ask this, but do you still have this wife?"

Casey was proud of herself that she'd managed to keep her voice almost steady as she asked the question. Though she wasn't sure she'd be able to stay upright, depending on the answer.

"I wouldn't have been with you if I did." Bonner's voice softened. "We got a divorce the year after I retired. It's been almost ten years now."

The relief nearly overwhelmed her. She wanted to wrap her arms around him, but she wasn't sure he'd be so receptive after she'd questioned him so relentlessly. "Why didn't you go back to the rodeo after the divorce if it had been only a year?"

"Because the old man had already hired me on here full-time. It was a good job with a steady paycheck. The sensible thing to do was stay here. Besides in rodeo every season there's some new kid there to take your place at the top of the rankings. I never wanted to be that aging has-been who didn't know when to quit."

A has-been…in his early twenties. Casey had trouble wrapping her head around that concept but she supposed bull riding was a young man's sport.

"Why didn't you just tell me all this to begin with instead of sneaking around?"

Bonner let out a snort. "Because no man likes to admit his mistakes."

She couldn't help but wonder what exactly he thought his mistake was. Retiring? The divorce? The marriage to begin with? Maybe all three.

It didn't matter. She rose from the mattress and walked to him.

"I'm sorry I pried. It was none of my business and I shouldn't have researched you online." She laid a hand on each of his shoulders.

He wrapped his arms around her waist and pulled her closer. "Nah. I shouldn't have made it such a big secret you felt you had to."

"It's okay." She took a step even closer, until they were pressed together. She rested her head on top of his. "Wanna have make-up sex now?"

"Yes." Bonner's laugh vibrated through her. "But not under the old man's roof."

"Like you said, the milk's already been spilt…quite a few times and places, if I remember correctly." Casey liked when Bonner's cowboy wisdom worked so neatly in her favor.

She felt him smile. "I guess you're right. Help me to the bed?"

"You're hurt that badly?" Casey let him pull himself up by grabbing her arm. "Jeez, are you sure you're going to be able to perform in this shape?"

"No, I'm not sure." His eyes flared like the devil was inside him. "You might have to do all the work."

She rolled her eyes at that idea but started to think he might be right when she got him to the bed. He crashed onto the mattress and lay, unmoving. He went to reach for one foot and cringed.

Flopping back again, he covered his face with his forearm. "Can you take off my boots?"

She could see his agony at feeling helpless. Casey moved to the end of the bed and tried to control her smile. "This is killing you, isn't it? Being hurt. Having to ask for help."

"Yup."

"But you must have been hurt all the time when you were riding. I've watched professional bull riding on television. I've seen the guys limping around." She spoke as she grabbed his boot and pulled.

He winced. "I was younger then."

"You're still young." She pulled the other boot off and actually got a pain-filled grunt from Bonner. After dropping the boot to the floor next to the bed, she lay down next to him. She saw the pain in his face. Maybe he was even worse than he'd let on. "Wanna just lay here for a few minutes?"

"God, yes." Bonner didn't even attempt to hide his relief.

Casey sat up against the headboard as Bonner looked like it was all he could do to lay still. "Hm, maybe I should have gone with Dakota and Justus to the bar."

"Oh, shut your pretty little mouth. I'll be fine… In a

minute."

She smiled, enjoying the teasing. Enjoying even more that Bonner was in her bed, even if they weren't having sex at the moment.

That they could joke with each other and talk about things was nice too. It proved this wasn't just some animal attraction between them.

Bonner turned just his head on the pillow to face her. "So, now you know about my past. You owe me something about yours. Spill."

Even though she figured he was trying to distract her so she didn't demand anything physically strenuous from him for a little while, Casey decided she did owe him a truth for a truth. He'd confessed something he didn't like to tell anyone. Her turn.

"I can't cook."

"That's your confession?" His forehead wrinkled. "I tell you I was married and divorced and ruined my career for a woman who still left me afterward and you tell me you can't cook?"

"Well, there's a little more to it." Casey turned to face him and launched into the story of Christmas morning the year she was eight. The Cowboy Cody doll. The pink Easy-Bake oven. And most importantly, the vow to grow up and be the best at whatever she did and to never use that damn oven, or any other oven, for the rest of her life.

By the end of her tale, Bonner's eyes were twinkling with laughter. "I take it back. That little confession is just about equal to mine."

She laughed. "It is?"

He nodded. "Yup. And it explains so much."

"Like what?"

"Like why you find me so irresistible." He grinned.

Casey rolled her eyes. "Don't let it go to your head. It's Cowboy Cody I had a schoolgirl crush on. You just happen to look a little bit like him. Actually, the resemblance pretty much ends at the blue shirt."

She wasn't about to admit the truth to Bonner, that he might as well be the childhood man of her dreams come to life. The man definitely didn't need his ego stroked that much.

"You mean the blue shirt of mine you stole from me?" He lifted a brow and looked a bit too self satisfied.

"I didn't steal it. You gave it to me and I'm keeping it. You have a whole case of them anyway." She crossed her arms, firm in her resolve. That shirt was coming home with her to New York as a memento even if she had to wrestle him for it.

Actually, wrestling could lead to some fun.

"That was before I knew you were only using me to fill your Cowboy Cody fetish. But yeah, I did give it to you. You can keep it. However, I bet I have something your Cowboy Cody didn't have."

"And what would that be?"

A devilish expression appeared on Bonner's sun-browned face. "Unbuckle my belt and I'll show you."

Casey narrowed her eyes. "Hm. I think you're enjoying the idea that I'll be doing all the work thanks to your injury."

"Well, I have an idea about that."

"Really. Do tell."

"Take off those pants of yours, spin yourself around and hop on up here." He grinned and patted his chest. "I'll be happy to show you what I have in mind."

She didn't need to have what he was suggesting spelled out. Her cowboy was a real creative problem solver and she wasn't about to argue with his solution.

The idea of his tongue on her, his mouth torturing her into orgasm, his long thick fingers plunging into her as she worked him with her mouth at the same time had Casey throbbing and he hadn't even touched her yet.

Reaching for the waist of her pants, she smiled. "Sounds good to me."

CHAPTER TWELVE

Casey couldn't believe the week was over. Just when she really didn't want to leave, she was sitting down to her last meal at the ranch—breakfast with Jake, Dakota, Justus and Bonner. Tomorrow they'd all still be here, but her seat would be empty. She glanced sideways at Bonner.

Would he even notice?

She shook that thought out of her head. Of course, he'd notice. They'd spent the past two nights in her bed together.

His injury aside, they'd pretty much taken each other every way imaginable. Their time together may have been short, but it sure was productive—in her bed, and on the desk in her room, even in the big old cast-iron bathtub.

That had begun strictly to see if a soak in a hot bath would help his muscles feel better. It wasn't her fault the hot, soapy water was too much of a temptation for both of them. That she'd ended up straddling Bonner, sliding down over him, hard and fast until the water splashed over the edge and on to the floor.

They'd soaked quite a few towels mopping it up, then had to drape them all over her room to dry before Mrs. Jones noticed.

But now it was over. Whatever had been between Bonner and her was over.

How could it continue with her in New York and him in Colorado? It was crazy to even consider trying. Besides, he hadn't said a word about trying to maintain any semblance of a relationship after she left. Maybe this was just a fling for him.

That's what it should be for her too. It wasn't.

"What time is your flight?"

She glanced up as Jake's question broke into her misery.

"Noon." Casey cleared the frog out of her throat that had made her voice unclear.

Jake nodded. "You've got plenty of time."

She forced a smile. "Yeah, I don't think the security lines at Yampa Valley Regional are quite as long as the ones I'm used to in the New York airports.

"No. Not quite. The bigger issue is if they close the security checkpoint while the only worker goes to get coffee or take a leak." Jake's hearty, gruff laugh never failed to make her smile.

Sometimes it was hard for Casey to remember Jake had two sides to him.

That even though the Jake she'd come to know was completely at home on the ranch, dressed in boots and jeans, his hat tipped back as he yelled across a pen of cattle to one of the guys, he was a hugely successful business man. The man who'd shepherded a multi-million dollar, multi-national, hundred-year-old corporation into the twenty-first century.

Or that Jake flew to the corporate headquarters in New York to check on the operations there monthly. She'd even heard he maintained a standing reservation at one of the better hotels bordering Central Park for his monthly trips.

The dichotomy was surreal.

She tried to picture Bonner in New York, her city, and found it nearly impossible.

He'd be like a fish out of water.

No, Bonner Blue Boyd belonged in a saddle on the back

of a horse. Riding the range, the wind in his face, his boots in the stirrups, the cattle at his feet, his dog Misty trailing behind.

His home, his life, was here.

Jeez, she was getting sappy. She couldn't help it. Like it or not, she was going to miss him. More than she wanted to admit.

She'd miss it all. After taking almost every meal in this room with these people, her two-room apartment in the city was going to feel even emptier.

Maybe she should get a cat for company. Or a dog. One like Misty. But what would she do with it when she had to travel for work?

Which brought up another concern—what was she going to do when she did come back here to the ranch for business?

Would she and Bonner pick back up where they'd left off? Fall right into bed like no time and distance had been between them? And what if she came back to find he'd gotten a girlfriend?

The bitter taste of bile crept into the back of her throat at that thought.

Bonner had been right. Don't mix business with pleasure. They should have stuck to his cowboy code and not given in to the attraction. Codes were codes for a reason.

Now... Well, now she'd have to deal with the consequences. She was afraid those could be pretty bad. Wearing his shirt while weeping on her sofa with a pint of ice cream and a spoon kind of bad.

The huge disappointment over Cowboy Cody when she was eight aside, Casey had lived twenty-eight years without a broken heart. One trip to the Maverick ranch may well break that winning streak.

Meanwhile Bonner ate his steak and eggs and drank his coffee, occasionally defending his mug from Jake's thievery, like this morning was no different than any other.

Maybe he wouldn't miss her after all.

"Well it's sure been a pleasure having you here, Miss Casey." Fork and knife in hand, Justus gazed at her over his meal.

Dakota nodded. "Yes, ma'am. It was a pleasure. You come back again real soon."

"Come back in February or March for calving season. You'd enjoy that. Seeing 'em born." Justus turned to Bonner. "Blue, don't you think she'd like that?"

Bonner glanced at her and then away again so fast, she nearly missed it. "I do."

Fighting what suspiciously felt like tears, Casey nodded. "I would like that. It sounds miraculous. We'll have to see what the corporate schedule looks like, I suppose."

Jake let out a snort. "You come back whenever you want to. We don't live by corporate schedules at this end of the business the way the square asses in the New York offices do."

She laughed. "Have you forgotten I'm one of them?"

"Nope. You may well be one of them, but you're one of us too. You've proven yourself here this week. Keeping up with the boys around here. Riding out with Bonner. Surviving a night in the cabin."

Jake's mention of the night she'd spent with Bonner had her heart aching. "Thanks, Jake."

"Oh, and I looked over that marketing plan you left for me. I like it. You've got a good head on your shoulders and a knack for all that stuff I've got no mind for myself. Maverick Western is lucky to have you."

Now she really did have to fight the tears. Validation from the old man himself was more than she'd dared hope for. "Thank you, sir. That means a lot to me."

Bonner, quieter than usual, didn't comment or even glance up as he scraped the last of the eggs off his plate.

Casey pushed her chair back from the table. If she didn't get out of this room, she'd break down bawling in front of the boss as well as the man who apparently wasn't affected at all by her leaving. "I still have to pack a few things."

Jake nodded. "If I don't see you before you leave, safe trip."

Dakota looked up. "Yes, ma'am. You have a safe journey."

"See you next time. Think some about calving season. You ain't truly experienced ranch life 'til you've spent a night in a calving barn." Justus grinned.

Bonner finally glanced up. He stood and extended his hand to her. Amazed that one of the most incredible weeks of her life was going to end with a handshake, she couldn't do much more than reach out her own hand and shake his.

"It was a pleasure working with you this week, Miss Casey."

Working? She swallowed hard. "You too."

Images flashed through her mind as she held his hand, so big and warm, in hers. She remembered how his touch had been all over her. His fingers knew every inch of her body, inside and out.

That was over. Now he was all business once again. Her chest actually hurt from that knowledge.

She pulled her hand out of his grasp. "I better...you know. Get ready."

With a nod he sat again and she walked as fast as she could without looking like she was fleeing, to the privacy of her room.

An hour later, earlier than she had to, she said goodbye to Mrs. Jones in the kitchen, and then loaded her bags into the trunk of the rental car. She'd rather wait at the airport than here amid all the painful memories.

She programmed the GPS for the airport, and was told to drive to the nearest recognized route.

Teary eyed, she laughed, reminded of her arrival here. It felt like a lifetime ago, and at the same time the week had flown by in the blink of an eye.

Casey glanced at the buildings in view, stupidly searching for one last glimpse of Bonner. She tried to reason away the pain.

Men were different. They didn't let themselves get

emotionally attached. It didn't mean he didn't care about her. Of course, he couldn't show emotion at the breakfast table anyway. Not with the others there. Their relationship, or fling, or whatever it was, had been secret.

A private good bye would have been nice though. She supposed the kiss he'd given her before slipping out of her bed about midnight last night was her good bye. Had she known that, perhaps she would have prolonged it a bit more.

With a sigh filled with regret, Casey put the car in gear and headed down the path she knew led toward the gate. It was a beautiful drive. She wished she could appreciate it more, but the myriad of emotions assaulting her didn't leave a whole lot of room for enjoying the scenery.

Casey wiped at a tear that crept from her eye. She would not allow herself to cry over a man.

Unfortunately, the second tear hadn't gotten that message.

As she dashed the tear away, something caught her attention in the rear view mirror. She slowed the car and squinted at the motion reflected in the small mirror until the dust took the form of a man and horse.

Heart pounding, Casey threw the car into park and opened the door. Bonner leapt from the saddle before the horse even stopped and strode toward where she stood next to the car.

He captured her in his arms before she could wrap her mind fully around his actions. His mouth covered hers, hard and demanding. He tangled his fingers in her hair, angling her head and driving his tongue between her lips.

When he finally broke away, he pulled her to him. He held her close, her head resting on his chest. "I couldn't let you leave without a proper good bye."

Against her cheek, through that stupid blue denim shirt she'd come to love, Casey felt his heart pounding. "I'm glad."

There was so much to say. So much she wanted him to say, but neither spoke a word.

He leaned back and, cupping her face in his hands, stared into her eyes. Somehow they didn't need words. She knew. He cared. He didn't want her to leave either. And, just like her, he'd realized there was nothing either of them could do about it. Her place was there. His, here.

He pressed his mouth to hers again in a poignant, too brief kiss. Then he reached around her and opened the driver's side door. She got in and while trying to memorize the look, feel, even smell of him, watched as he slammed the door, closing her in.

She didn't lower the window. They were done. There was nothing more to say. With a forced smile, she glanced one more time at Bonner and with a hand that shook shifted the car into gear.

As she drove away, she saw him in the rear view mirror. He stood in the road and didn't move. She watched until she couldn't see him any more.

CHAPTER THIRTEEN

"That is one magnificent turkey, Mrs. Jones." Jake looked like he was starting to salivate just from the sight of it.

Though that could also be from the fact he and Mrs. Jones had struck a deal. Just for this meal he was allowed to eat whatever he wanted—in moderation—even if it was against his diet.

"It should be. I started cooking it at sunrise. Oops, forgot the gravy." She turned back toward the kitchen.

Jake scowled and leaned in closer to Bonner. "Yeah. Spoiled my morning, she did. I snuck down early to steal a cup of real coffee from the pot and she was already in there stuffing the damn bird."

Bonner grinned. "Don't worry. Tomorrow things will be back to normal and you'll be back to stealing coffee again."

"Can't come soon enough for me."

Mrs. Jones appeared again, carrying a gravy boat. "Here you go."

"Aren't you going to sit and join us?" Jake lifted one snowy brow.

"I've been tasting things all day. I don't need to eat."

He screwed up his mouth. "Then just sit there and pick.

Don't you want to see me enjoying your cooking?"

"Come to think of it, I better sit. Have to make sure you don't stuff yourself or the doctor will be hollering next time he tests your cholesterol."

It was a dance the two had every year on Thanksgiving. Christmas too. Mrs. Jones, a widow, was always here cooking for the ranch on the holidays. Jake would always ask her to join them. They'd banter back and forth about it for a little while until finally Mrs. Jones went to the kitchen and got herself a place setting.

Bonner wouldn't know what to do if they didn't stick to the tradition. It had been going on for so long.

He had always found Thanksgivings at the Maverick ranch interesting. Who would be at the table was usually up for grabs.

Some years there were cowboys in town for one thing or another, far from home and alone. The old man would always include them in the meal if they had nowhere else to go.

Some years, though not often, members of the Maverick family would be there—Jake's grandson or granddaughter and more recently their spouses and kids.

And some years, like this year, it was just him and the old man.

"Where'd Justus and Dakota head off to again?" Jake reached for the bowl of mashed potatoes.

"Colorado Springs. Some Thanksgiving rodeo." Bonner stabbed a turkey leg with his fork and pulled it onto his plate.

"Ah, that's right." With a glance at the door, the old man scooped a second heaping spoonful of buttery potatoes onto his plate.

Bonner hid his smile. It was probably the thrill of getting away with something that drove Jake, more than his love of foods he wasn't supposed to eat. "Family couldn't make it out this year?"

"Nah. There's always something going on with the kids that keep them from traveling. Recitals. Sports." He shrugged. "Wasn't like that back in my day."

"Wasn't like that in my day either." Bonner laughed.

Mrs. Jones returned, plate, napkin, knife and fork in hand. "Well it's a damn shame, if you ask me. Family should be together on Thanksgiving."

Bonner let out a sigh as guilt struck him.

"Stop looking like a sad puppy. I wasn't talking about you, Bonner. Your mother moved away from you. You didn't move away from her."

"How is your mom?" Jake glanced at Bonner, before his attention was drawn back to the casserole dish filled with stuffing.

"She's doing good. I called her this morning. She says it's beautiful and sunny in Florida and she and her boyfriend are going to have dinner at the restaurant on the golf course." Bonner shrugged.

He couldn't feel badly about that. His father had died years before and much too young. He was happy his mother could find someone to spend her later years with.

But that didn't mean he could pick up and leave the farm to fly to Florida and stay in her condo on the golf course on holidays. He had a life and a job here.

He had family here too, blood or not. He glanced at Jake and Mrs. Jones. "Everything is great, Mrs. Jones."

She dismissed the compliment with a wave of her hand. "You say that all the time."

"Because it's true all the time." Bonner smiled.

"So tomorrow is Maverick Western's first Black Friday Promotion."

Jake's announcement had Bonner frowning and laughing at the same time. "Congratulations. Now what's that mean?"

"It means our girl Miss Casey has been busy during her first month with us and tomorrow, we'll see if it pays off."

The mention of Casey had Bonner paying more attention. His heart rate sped faster. He'd asked Jake about her and how she was doing in the new job a few times, until he decided he was starting to appear too interested in her.

"Then I hope it does."

"Oh, that reminds me. She wants you and the boys to start taking pictures of what you're doing every day. She wants you to tweet them." The old man laughed so hard after making that announcement he began to cough.

Bonner halted the motion of his fork halfway to his mouth. "Tweet them?"

"Yup. She says she'll send a memo with all the information." Jake focused completely on his food, making Bonner think Jake didn't know how the hell to tweet any more than he did.

Meanwhile, Bonner had to stifle a groan at the word memo. It had been where he'd first seen Casey's name written only a month ago. Little did he know then she'd have such an effect on him. That he'd still be thinking about her now.

Mrs. Jones shook her head. "You two men. I swear. Still stuck in the last century. Twitter is where you can post what you're doing on the Internet so everyone in the world can see."

"Why would everyone in the world care what I'm doing everyday?" Bonner's frown deepened.

She shrugged. "Beats me, but it seems millions of people are doing it."

"How do you know all this stuff?" Jake stared at Mrs. Jones.

"Besides the fact I live in this century? They were talking about it on some talk show I had on while I was polishing the silver."

"We have silver?" The old man frowned.

"What do you think you're eating off of right now? I always bring it out on holidays."

Jake looked down at the fork in his hand. "Hm."

She shook her head again. "Not sure why I bother."

Bonner smiled. "I noticed the silver, Mrs. Jones. It's very nice...and shiny."

"Thank you, Blue." After delivering a sweet smile to Bonner, she sent a nasty look at Jake.

"Kiss ass." Jake spoke the words beneath his breath in Bonner's general direction before he pushed his plate away from him. "Wow. I'm stuffed. What's for dessert?"

"If you're stuffed, why do you wanna know about dessert?" Mrs. Jones cocked one eyebrow at the old man.

"Because for today, you can't yell at me for having some so I'm eating it."

She rolled her eyes. "Pumpkin Pie."

"Homemade?"

"Of course, homemade. When have I ever in all the years I've worked here fed you store bought pie?"

"Just checking." Jake pushed his chair back from the table. "After we help carry this back into the kitchen, wanna watch some football until dessert's ready?"

"Sounds good." Bonner stood. He'd been considering seconds on the turkey and potatoes, but since there was Mrs. Jones's pumpkin pie, hopefully with fresh whipped cream, he'd save room.

The old man surprised him by slapping him on the back and pulling him into a one-armed hug. "Glad you're here, son."

Bonner hid his surprise at the old man's sudden show of affection. "Nowhere I'd rather be."

He nodded. "Me either. Cut from the same piece of leather, me and you."

"Yes, sir."

Jake's familiar saying brought Bonner right back to that day with Casey when he'd said those very words about Dakota and Justus and she'd started to take notes.

Damn. Nothing was safe anymore.

Even the littlest things triggered a memory of her and, hard as he tried, he couldn't hold them back.

Should he contact her? Wait for her to come back to the ranch for work? Go out and find a woman to take his mind off her?

That last idea left him cold.

He sighed. One day he was going to have to figure out

what to do about it, but not today. Today was for food and football and family—even if they weren't blood.

Bonner picked up the turkey platter, still heavily laden with the carcass, and turned toward the kitchen.

They'd be eating good on leftovers tomorrow—if the old man didn't eat them all up tonight after Mrs. Jones went to bed.

Jake picked up the bowl of potatoes and then put it back down, grabbing the edge of the table and leaning heavily.

Bonner paused near the kitchen doorway. "You all right?"

"Yeah. Fine. Just got indigestion from all that food is all."

"Told you not to eat too much." Mrs. Jones's voice came from inside the kitchen.

"Ears like a hawk that one." Jake rubbed his chest.

"You go and sit and find the game on TV. I'll finish cleaning up here and meet you in there." Bonner knew something was not quite right with the old man when he gave in without an argument and headed for the TV room.

He'd keep an eye on him tonight, then tomorrow, if he didn't feel better, they could call the doctor.

Satisfied with that plan, Bonner turned toward the kitchen door.

CHAPTER FOURTEEN

"Casey, you can't stay home alone and work. It's Thanksgiving."

"Yes, Jody. I know. I figured that out when I turned on the television and saw all those giant balloons floating down 34th Street."

Casey put her laptop down on the coffee table in front of the sofa and pulled her legs up beneath the hem of Bonner's shirt.

She'd worn it to sleep every night since leaving Colorado. She'd eventually given in and washed it, but for a solid two weeks at least, she'd gone to sleep and woken up surrounded by the scent of him.

Pulling the plaid throw over her, she snuggled deeper into the cushions, settling in for a long conversation with her sister. "Maverick Western's first Black Friday promotion launches tomorrow. I have to make sure everything's on track."

"But it's a holiday today." Jody apparently had no other argument besides that.

Casey laughed. "It's also the most important day of the entire year in retail tomorrow."

"Just come for dinner. You don't have to stay late. We're eating early." Jody paused and then added, "Mom and Dad aren't coming."

Casey had been about to bow out, once and for all, when her sister had delivered that killing blow. "What? Why not?"

"They had an invitation to dinner with Dad's boss."

Well, well, well.

There were very few things that could tempt Casey to make the drive to Connecticut from the city, especially during the dark days of winter when the sun set at like four in the afternoon. She would be perfectly happy to stay snuggled under the Maverick Western blanket, order dinner to be delivered, and work on her laptop in front of the TV.

But the information her sister had let drop opened up a new temptation.

"Mom and Dad are going to have dinner with Dad's boss on Thanksgiving rather than with their children and grandchildren? On Thanksgiving." Casey knew she was repeating herself, but she couldn't believe her ears.

Her mother, Mrs. Perfect, the one who was so quick with the lectures about all that Casey did wrong by missing family holidays for work and not serving up her fair share of Harrington grandchildren, was actually missing Thanksgiving at Jody's house.

"Yup." Jody delivered that one word and was silent.

Wow.

Casey drew in a deep breath and asked, "What time is dinner?"

"Four."

"Okay. I'll bring the wine."

"Great. See you then." There was a smile in Jody's voice, but Casey didn't care if her sister was feeling victorious she'd won.

Casey hung up with the satisfaction of knowing that she was one up on her mother. At least for today.

She had work to do but she had an hour until she needed to leave.

It wasn't like she was going to get all dressed up to go to her sister's house for dinner. A sweater, skinny jeans and a pair of high leather boots would be fine. So she still had time to get a little bit of work done before getting ready to go.

Besides, this particular work had to do with Bonner so she had no complaints about doing it.

Casey needed to write him and the boys instructions on how to send pictures from their cell phones—when they had signal—directly to the Maverick Western social media accounts.

It was all part of the social networking platform for her marketing plan. What customer could resist the lure of real live cowboys? And the more often they were exposed to the Maverick name, and the longer they stayed on the Maverick sites, the more product they'd eventually buy.

Hell, just seeing Bonner in this blue shirt had made her want it for herself. She'd barely been able to take it off since arriving home.

Of course, she was a special case, because with this shirt came some pretty impactful memories.

The customers would just have to come up with their own cowboy fantasies. One look at Bonner, Justus and Dakota riding the horses with Misty at their heels, and the buyer would be hooked. The men would envy the pure manliness and freedom. The women...well they'd just want them.

That in mind, Casey's fingers flew over the keys.

Glancing up sometime later, the clock in the corner of her screen proved she'd worked so intently crafting the perfect instructional page for Bonner and the boys, she'd lost track of the day.

"Shit." She flipped the lid on the laptop closed and scrambled to throw on some makeup and an outfit.

After grabbing two bottles from the wine rack on the way to the door, she headed out.

The drive wasn't too bad. It was a sunny afternoon, something she might not have noticed if her sister hadn't talked her into coming and she'd remained sequestered in her apartment for the day.

There wasn't much traffic between the city and Connecticut. Casey supposed she'd gotten on the road too late for that. Most people were probably at their families' by now, already being tortured by their own relatives.

But today at Jody's house should be nice. No mother there to drop passive-aggressive comments about Casey not being married yet or not having a boyfriend. No father to politely inquire about her job even though his gaze stayed glued to the football game on television as he nodded and pretended to listen to her answer. Just Jody, her husband Kent, and their two perfect daughters, Jenna and Courtney. That, Casey could handle.

As she pulled up to her sister's split level ranch in the suburbs and saw the door open and the two girls run out before she'd even gotten her car door open, Casey had to smile.

Her nieces didn't care that she wasn't married and didn't have kids. They didn't give her the cold shoulder when she was traveling for business and had to miss a family event. To them, she was the coolest aunt on earth.

"Aunt Casey!" Jenna crashed into Casey's stomach and wrapped both arms around her. Courtney followed seconds later.

Luckily their eight and ten year old bodies weren't heavy enough to knock Casey over with the full body tackle.

She did hold the wine bottles a bit tighter so she wouldn't drop them and bathe the driveway in Beaujolais Nuveau. "Hey, you two. I missed you."

"Me too. We want you to tell us all about the cowboy ranch." Courtney practically bounced with excitement.

"It was a cattle ranch." Casey laughed, though Courtney wasn't exactly wrong. There sure had been one hell of a cowboy there. The familiar feeling of longing settled in her chest. She pushed it aside. "In fact, I think I might even have a few pictures on my cell phone, if you want to see..."

"Yay! I wanna see." Courtney led the way to the house

with something that looked like a half skip, half jog.

Casey wished she had half the energy these girls did. Though she supposed back when she was eight, she didn't just walk anywhere either.

Jody laughed in the doorway. "Glad you're here. They haven't stopped talking about Aunt Casey all day. I thought Kent was going to lose his mind if he had to tell them again how many more minutes until you arrived."

Casey laughed and waved at Kent where he squatted in front of the fireplace, putting in a log. "Hey, Kent. Happy Thanksgiving."

"You too, Aunt Casey." He smiled. "Let's pop that wine."

Jody grabbed the bottles from Casey. "I'm on it. Turkey will be ready in a few minutes."

"Sorry, I didn't get here earlier. I tried to get some work done before I left and lost track of time."

"Oh, don't worry. The girls will make up for any lost time, I'm sure." Kent closed the fireplace's screen and brushed his hands together. "So how was Colorado? You survived ranch life, I see."

"It was actually really great." Did her cheeks look as red as they felt? Casey still couldn't manage to think about the ranch without blushing, even a month later.

"Aunt Casey, sit next to me." Jenna bounced onto the couch cushion.

Courtney frowned. "No, she has to sit between us. I wanna see pictures of the cowboys."

Casey glanced at the girls. Courtney, at least, seemed to have inherited her cowboy fetish. Perhaps it was genetic. "You'll both get to see. Don't worry."

"Well heck, if there's pictures of cowboys, I wanna see them too." Jody carried out three glasses of wine from the kitchen.

"Oh really? This is new. I seem to remember someone— *Jody*—trying to talk me out of asking Santa for the Cowboy Cody doll for Christmas." Casey leaned close to Courtney. "Your mom wanted me to ask for a Barbie instead back when

I was your age."

"Who'd rather have a Barbie than a cowboy?" Courtney screwed up her mouth dramatically.

On the other side of Casey, Jenna shook her head. "No, Barbie's way cooler. She's got all those fun clothes."

Casey shot Jody a look. "Jenna's definitely your daughter."

"If I hadn't given birth to her, I'd wonder if Courtney is yours." Jody raised a brow. "So speaking of cowboys...did you meet anyone interesting on your business trip?"

"I met quite a few interesting people." Casey concentrated on the wine glass in her hand.

"Oh my God. You met a man."

"What?" Casey's attention snapped to her sister. She tried to look innocent and rolled her eyes. "No. Why do you say that?"

"You're blushing. And you can't hold eye contact."

Casey forced herself to look at Jody, and found her sister grinning from ear to ear.

"There's nothing to talk about." Casey shook her head, but she couldn't help the smile that crept onto her lips just from the thought of Bonner.

"Oh, that's it. You're going to spill it all. Come into the kitchen with me. We're going to talk." Jody reached down and grabbed Casey's hand, pulling her off the couch.

Jenna and Courtney jumped up to follow. "You girls stay here and help your father watch the fire."

Kent's eyebrows rose. He glanced at the single log, barely burning. "Um, yeah. I could use the help."

"But she's going to show us pictures." Courtney stamped her little foot and Casey couldn't help but smile, knowing she'd done that at her age. Hell, she still did it sometimes.

Resigned now, Casey gave in. "My phone is right here in my purse. You can look at the pictures while your mom and I go...check on the turkey."

When Jody was after something, she could be relentless. She'd have to feed her sister some details about meeting Bonner, but definitely not all of them. No way. Her cheeks heated at the thought.

Casey located the pictures of the ranch on the phone. The first picture was of Bonner with Misty. She'd taken it the day before she left. Just looking at his picture, his blue eyes piercing under the brim of his hat, took Casey's breath away.

She handed the phone to Courtney. "Here you go. Make sure to share with your sister."

"I will." Wide-eyed, she cradled the phone in both hands and stared at the screen.

Jody glanced over her daughter's shoulder at the picture of the cowboy in the blue shirt with the black and white dog. "That him?"

Casey let out a laugh. It was no use trying to hide it. "Yeah."

"Kitchen. Now." Jody spun on one heel and strode to the doorway.

Kent stood to come look over the girls' shoulders. He raised one brow when he saw the picture. "You really do have a cowboy fetish, don't you?"

As Casey watched Courtney become totally engrossed in the photo of Bonner, even zooming in on it to see him closer, Casey laughed. "I wouldn't get so cocky if I were you. Apparently so does your daughter."

"Daddy. Can we go to Colorado?" Courtney glanced up as Jenna tried to grab the phone.

"Yeah, I'm starting to see that." He grimaced and then leaned down closer to his daughters. "We'll talk about it later. Now what other pictures does Aunt Casey have on there? Are there any cows?"

Smiling, Casey made her exit, only to find Jody tapping her foot in the kitchen waiting for her. "So…"

"So his name is Bonner. He's a former state rodeo champion and now he runs the Maverick ranch. He's an honest to goodness cowboy, Jody. He straps on his spurs and chaps and hops on a horse to head to work in the morning the way most men grab their briefcases and get on the subway." Now that Casey had started to talk about Bonner, it seemed she couldn't stop.

"Age?"

"Early thirties."

"Single?" Jody was like a prosecutor and Casey was the hostile witness on the stand.

"Divorced ten years ago. He got married young. She made him quit rodeo at the peak of his career and then left him." Casey found it very easy to be jealous of the woman Bonner had given his name to, and she'd never been the jealous type. Interesting.

"Is he looking to get married again?"

That question gave Casey pause. "I don't know."

Jody studied Casey intently for a moment. "Are *you* interested in getting married?"

Casey opened her mouth to give her rote answer—the one she'd been giving friends, relatives and colleagues for most of her life—that she was focusing on her career. But it seemed she couldn't say the words today.

"Oh my God. You are!" Jody had never looked happier.

Sputtering, Casey didn't know what to say to undo the damage. Before she knew it, Jody would likely have their mother on the phone announcing her engagement to a man she'd had a week of incredible sex with but hadn't spoken to since.

She took a steadying breath and gathered her thoughts. "Jody. First of all even considering a relationship with him would be nuts. He's a real live cowboy. I'm a New Yorker."

Jody pursed her lips while considering that and then nodded. "I am having some trouble picturing you living on a ranch. And you'd probably die if you were away from the city for too long."

The truth hurt a little too much. She and Bonner were from two different worlds and because of that would never be together for more than casual sex a few times a year when she visited the ranch.

Casey needed to lighten this conversation before Jody saw that she'd already started to fall for a man she had no future with.

"You don't know the half of it. You should have seen me using the outhouse," Casey joked.

Jody nearly spit her mouthful of wine out at that. "That I would pay to see. All right, so I see the difficulties. But tell me you at least had a little fun with him. I'm sure your cowboy, unlike that Cody doll you wanted, was anatomically correct. Right?"

"Jody!" Shocked, Casey still couldn't stop the grin. "And yeah. He was. Very."

They were both giggling when Kent came into the room carrying Casey's phone. He handed it to her. "A text just came through, Casey."

"Thanks." She opened the text and as she read the words, the whole world seemed to tilt.

"Everything all right?" Jody touched her arm.

"Um, it's a confidential message from the CFO of Maverick Western. He needs me to write an official press release ASAP." Casey put her wine down and leaned on the kitchen counter. Feeling in shock, she glanced up at her sister and her husband. "Jake Maverick died today of a massive coronary."

CHAPTER FIFTEEN

Dazed, Bonner sat in a leather chair in the waiting room of the offices of Stern & Wiseman—Jake's attorney.

The days following Jake's sudden death had passed in a surreal swirling mash-up of events, beginning with Bonner finding him lying on the sofa in front of the television Thanksgiving Day and culminating now, with his summons for the reading of the will.

"Mr. Boyd."

Bonner glanced up to find a balding man wearing a suit extending a hand toward him. "Yes, sir."

"Harold Stern. I'm Jake's attorney. It's a pleasure to meet you. Jake spoke very fondly of you."

Not really knowing how to respond to that, Bonner simply shook the man's hand and nodded.

"Come on in to my office. The others aren't scheduled to arrive for a while yet." The attorney turned and led the way into a paneled office dominated by a wall of books and a huge wooden desk. "Please. Have a seat."

There was plenty of seating to choose from, from the leather sofa to the two chairs that matched the one Mr. Stern lowered himself into behind the desk.

"I understand you were the person who found him?"

Bonner glanced up at the question. He had to swallow the lump from his throat before he could even attempt an answer. The loss of Jake was still too fresh. "Um, yeah. After dinner Thanksgiving Day."

He'd finished helping Mrs. Jones with the leftovers and had gone to find the old man in the TV room. Jake was lying on the sofa.

It had looked as if he were asleep, but when Bonner tried to wake him to watch the game and have the pie he'd been so excited about, he realized something was very wrong.

"No one else was there?"

"Not in the room with me, no. But Mrs. Jones, the housekeeper, was right in the kitchen." Bonner frowned.

Surely the man wasn't accusing him of something. Another thought hit him—why was he here before the rest of Jake's family? Hell, why was he here for the reading of the will at all?

"Mrs. Jones was the only other one in the house at the time?"

"Yes, sir. The other hands who usually take meals with us were away that day." Bonner may not have much experience with attorneys or even wills, but each question the lawyer asked increased his suspicion that something was odd here.

"No family members were at the ranch visiting for the holiday?"

"No." Feeling defensive, Bonner sat straighter in his seat. "What's this about, Mr. Stern?"

The man narrowed his eyes for a moment before he answered. "Jake came to me about a month ago. He wanted to make changes to his will. Major changes. I wasn't sure I agreed with him at the time, but I'm beginning to think I was wrong."

Mr. Stern stood and walked around to the front of the desk. He pushed the button on a flat screen television Bonner hadn't noticed hanging on the wall. "Jake made a video while he was here with the instructions that upon his death it would be shown to you, in private."

Bonner lifted a brow. A video? To be watched by him alone?

"Uh, all right."

He drew in a deep breath as Mr. Stern hit another button and Jake's image appeared on the screen.

The first sound of the old man's voice had Bonner's eyes beginning to blur with unshed tears. He blinked the misty haze away and tried to concentrate on what Jake was saying.

"...if you're watching this, it means I've finally kicked the bucket. I'm hoping at least I was doing something fun at the time. If not, feel free to make up a good story for the boys."

Bonner smiled, even as he wiped at his eyes.

"Anyway, there's something I probably should have told you long ago. Hell, I should of told your father too, long before we lost him to the cancer, but I guess it's too late for regrets. Anyway, most everyone involved is dead now so I think it's time you know the truth.

"A long time ago, believe it or not, I was a young handsome man. A real charmer. At that time, my father's ranch manager was Michael Boyd. One day he came home with a pretty young thing. Sara Bonner was her name and he was planning on marrying her. Well, Sara and I, let's just say we took a shine to each other and we did things we shouldn't. A week before the wedding she found out she was pregnant. There was no question the baby was mine but she wouldn't even consider shaming her family by backing out of the wedding and admitting the truth. She married Michael as planned and never told him that their only child John, your father, was really my son."

As Bonner sat stunned, Jake laughed on camera. "Damn baby came out looking so much like a Maverick I couldn't believe everyone didn't see it. But people see what they want to, I guess.

"Anyway, I went away to school for a few years. Eventually, ten years or so later, I got over Sara enough to find a woman I could spend my life with and I married her.

Josephine Smith was sweet as pie for every one of the years she walked this earth. She gave me Jake Junior the year we married. Then you know the rest. Junior, God rest his soul, married and gave us our first grandkids, Jake the third—J.J.—and Jocelyn. And eventually, they made me a great-grandpa three times over now. But what you never knew was that you're my grandson too, Bonner, and you have been since the day you came out of your mama all blue and gasping for life. I was there in the hospital the day you were born. My first grandchild, though no one knew it. And of all my blood kin, you're the one who's stuck close your whole life. You're a true Maverick, in blood and in your heart. Remember that, when the others try to push you around, and I'm sure they will. Never forget, you're a Maverick even if you don't carry the name."

The screen went black but Bonner kept staring at it, trying to take it all in. Finally, he turned to the lawyer. "This is all true?"

"According to Jake, it is."

"How can he be so sure my father was his son?"

The lawyer shrugged. "He wouldn't say, but he was unwavering on that point. Although I don't think it mattered whether or not you are his blood. You live on the ranch. He's known you since the day you were born. You've been working for him for years. You spent more time with him than any of his family members. It's obvious it's because of all that he named you in the will."

That brought Bonner's head up. "I'm named in the will?"

"Yes, you are. I can't give any specifics until the others arrive for the reading, but I will tell you this, I expect J.J. and Jocelyn might try to contest it."

"Contest it?" This was all more than Bonner could absorb. He shook his head. "They can have it all. I don't need anything. I don't want the old man's money. Hell, all I want is to keep my job running the herd. I don't need anything more than that."

"Maybe that's just it, Mr. Boyd. Jake was afraid if the

grandchildren have complete control of the future of the estate, there might not be a herd to run any longer. He was afraid they'd sell."

"The ranch has been in the family since Jake's grandfather's time." Bonner couldn't wrap his head around the idea. The Maverick ranch had been a part of the Colorado landscape for generations.

"And Jake knew you'd appreciate that history and do anything you could to preserve it."

Bonner nodded. Seeing a "For Sale" sign on the Maverick gate would break his heart. He wouldn't let that happen.

All right, so Jake must have left him part of the ranch. Okay. That he could handle. He'd just tell J.J. and Jocelyn he'd run it for them the best he could. He could forward their share of any profits to them. Though the way ranching went, it was by stashing away the profits from the good years that sometimes was the only thing to keep you afloat in the lean years. He'd have to convince them of that. Running a ranch wasn't like running a corporation like Maverick Western.

"You all right, Mr. Boyd?"

"Yeah. It's a lot to take in, is all." Bonner was barely aware of the distant sound of a door slamming.

"I know it is." The lawyer drew in a deep breath. "Well brace yourself, because the others are here. Oh, and one more thing. Don't be surprised if they demand a DNA test. My advice to you is to not offer it up willingly. Make them go through the Surrogate Court to get it."

Confused, reeling, and dreading the storm that was about to come, Bonner blew out a long slow breath. "All right."

A possible court battle against cousins he never even knew he had. DNA tests. A video confession. Just last week Bonner's biggest worry had been if they'd cut enough hay to last the herd for winter. Well that, and how soon Maverick Western's sexy little Director of Marketing would be traveling back to the ranch. Now…now his whole world was changed.

Mr. Stern slipped into the outer office and returned much too soon with Jake's grandson and granddaughter. They'd both just arrived in Colorado today, so this was the first time he'd seen them since Jake's passing.

Bonner stood and extended his hand to each in turn. "J.J., Jocelyn. I'm very sorry for your loss."

J.J. nodded. "Bonner. Good to see you again. Just wish it were under better circumstances."

Jocelyn smiled sweetly. "It's very nice that my grandfather included you in his will. I know you meant a lot to him. I wonder what he left you. I bet it was that horse of his. He had a real fondness for that horse. What was his name again?"

"Hercules. And actually we had to put him down about two years ago. Nearly killed Jake, losing him, but it was time. I picked him up a beautiful Paint to replace him, but it wasn't the same." Bonner watched Jocelyn lose interest about halfway through his story about the horse.

"Oh, well then I don't know what he could have left you, but I'm sure whatever it is, it's lovely." She perched her suit-clad behind on the leather sofa and turned toward the lawyer, and Bonner was more than happy he wasn't required to speculate further. He had a feeling Jocelyn was not going to be happy with today's revelations.

"So, shall we get on with it?" J.J. sat in the other chair next to Bonner. "We left both my daughter and Jocelyn's two children with my wife Kara back at the ranch."

"All right, let's get right down to it." The lawyer slid on a pair of glasses and referred to the paper on his desk. "I, Jacob John Maverick, being of sound mind and body, hereby devise, bequeath and grant all my real property as follows: forty-nine percent of the homestead currently known as Maverick Ranch, including all deeded acreage, buildings, equipment, livestock, water rights and all leases to grazing land, to be shared equally between my grandson, Jacob John Maverick the third and my granddaughter, Jocelyn Josephine Maverick Montgomery. The remaining fifty-one percent and controlling interest including all decision making power will go to my grandson Bonner Michael Boyd."

There was a gasp from Jocelyn. "What?"

She looked from the lawyer to her brother, to Bonner, who'd been prepared and had braced himself for something like this.

"In addition," The lawyer continued reading, the only indication he'd heard Jocelyn being the slight increase in his volume. "I do further bequest all my personal property to Bonner Boyd, including my share of Maverick Western, Inc. and its profits. I name Bonner Boyd my successor as President of Maverick Western, Inc. The remaining family members will retain all currently owned shares..."

His eyes wide, Bonner's gaze snapped to the lawyer. The old man hadn't just left him control of the ranch, but control of the company too?

What the hell had he been thinking? Bonner didn't know shit about running a company. Had Jake started to go soft in the head near the end?

"...Those known to the world as my family have strayed too far from the original concept of John Maverick whose genius and hard work founded this corporation over one hundred years ago. Bonner is the man I was at his age and he is the best man to represent Maverick Western and lead the company into continued success for the next hundred years. The future of Maverick Western, and the decisions from here forward, lie in Bonner's hands. The great-grandchildren will be taken care of with trusts set up for their education and future in the following amounts..."

The document went on to list the names of the three great-grandchildren and the amount of the trusts, but Bonner was pretty sure the children's parents didn't hear a word of it. They sat in shocked silence.

When the lawyer stopped reading, J.J. laughed bitterly and shook his head. "I knew I should have been around more. This is his way of punishing us for not living the kind of life he wanted us to."

"No, I think someone's been influencing his decisions. Someone close enough to him to convince a lonely old man he was actually his grandson." Jocelyn shot Bonner a look ripe with accusation.

Mr. Stern removed his glasses. "Jake had a feeling you'd react like this. He wanted me to assure you that Mr. Boyd knew nothing of his blood connection to the family or his being named in the will until he was informed today and that Mr. Boyd has never enacted any undue influence upon him. In fact, I think Jake's exact words, or near enough were, 'that boy does nothing but keep his head down, work hard and try to live his life the best way he can. He's a true Maverick and he'll run things right.'"

Bonner bowed his head and closed his eyes as emotions threatened to overtake him.

"And I may be out of line here, but I have to say this," Mr. Stern continued. "Jake was a friend as well as a client, for many years. The only person in this room, the only soul named in this will I've seen show any emotion or grief over Jake's loss is Mr. Boyd. In my mind, that says something. So does the fact he spent Thanksgiving, and from what I was told, all holidays with Jake at the ranch when the rest of his family was absent."

Jocelyn drew in a sharp breath, as if the lawyer's words physically stung.

"My sister and I will want DNA proof." J.J. crossed his arms and shot Bonner a look.

Mr. Stern nodded. "Of course. It's your right to request the court subpoena a sample of Mr. Boyd's DNA for comparison to Jake's. I held the reading of the will before Jake's internment because I expected you might. Though I'd be remiss to not point out the *in terrorem* clause. It says that should you contest the will and lose, you forfeit your entire portion of the estate. Furthermore, even if you do successfully contest the will, Colorado's intestacy laws will still apply."

Bonner stared at the attorney, who might as well have been speaking a foreign language.

Mr. Stern continued, "That provides that even if the will is discredited and thrown out of Surrogate Court, the next of kin by marriage, adoption *or blood* inherit. That means if a DNA sample proves Mr. Boyd is blood, he will still inherit. Knowing that, will you both still be contesting?"

"So you're saying if we contest the will and lose, we lose absolutely everything to him. And even if we win, but DNA proves he's blood, he *still* gets his share?"

"That's correct." Mr. Stern nodded. "And keep in mind, the law requires the wishes of the testator be honored, unless it's proven that he lacked the mental capacity. So to win, you'll have to prove in court that Jake Maverick, a man well-known and respected in both the business and the ranching worlds, was mentally incapable at the time this will was drawn one month ago. Do you still want to take this to court, Mr. Maverick?"

"No, Mr. Stern. I, for one, won't be contesting the will." Scowling, J.J. glanced at his sister.

A stricken expression on her face, Jocelyn shook her head. "Neither will I."

"The old man sure got the last laugh, didn't he?" J.J. stood and let out a snort. "I can tell you this. It's a damn good thing we at least got a share of the ranch, because with an uneducated cowboy at the helm, Maverick Western is as good as sunk."

As hurtful as those words were, the only thing J.J. had done was voice out loud what Bonner feared himself deep down. How the hell was he going to pull this off?

Bonner arrived back at the ranch still in a daze. He found Mrs. Jones standing in the front hall, arms crossed. "Well, well, well. Got any instructions for me, boss?"

He lifted a brow. "You heard?"

"Couldn't avoid hearing. First J.J. called his wife and told her all about it. He must have called from the car because it weren't but fifteen minutes after the time they were to meet with the lawyer. Then Jocelyn got on J.J.'s cell phone and said to get the kids ready, they wouldn't be spending the night under this roof now that it belonged to a lying imposter. They swooped in here and stormed off for a hotel."

Mr. Stern had been right to suspect they wouldn't take it well. Hell, Bonner wasn't handling it that great himself. He'd stopped at the bar in town and downed a shot and a beer before heading home, just to be able to deal with it all.

It was crazy. Though Mrs. Jones seemed just fine with the sudden revelation of his Maverick bloodline.

He looked at her. "So you know it all, then?"

"Yup."

"And only fifty-one percent of the ranch belongs to me, not the whole thing," Bonner corrected. God, this was surreal.

"Yeah, I heard that too. And how if they demanded a test they could end up losing it all. Said it wasn't worth the gamble." Mrs. Jones's tone and expression of disgust told him her low opinion of J.J. and Jocelyn. "I can tell you this. I've been here a very long time and I don't need no stinking test to tell me you're a Maverick. I think you don't either."

"I don't know anything anymore." He shook his head and sunk onto the bench along the wall in the front hall. "What am I gonna do?"

Mrs. Jones frowned. "What do you mean, what are you gonna do? You're gonna be the man Jake knew you to be. You're gonna run this ranch the way you always have."

"And what about Maverick Western? He named me president. What do I know about that?"

"You're sharp. You'll learn. Besides, I know somebody who's pretty good at this business stuff, and she happens to be on your side in all this."

Bonner glanced up. "Who?"

"Miss Casey. She called here, you know. Said she was going to fly in for the funeral tomorrow except that J.J. had a memo sent out to all employees saying it was a small private service for family only. Bastard." She moved closer and pulled an envelope out of the pocket of her apron.

Once he'd recovered from both the shock of Mrs. Jones cussing and the mention of Casey's name, Bonner took the envelope and read his name written across it in feminine script. In the return address he saw *Casey Harrington* and a New York City address. His instincts told him to read it in private.

He stashed the envelope in his jacket pocket. "I'm going to have to go to the New York headquarters."

The only thing that made him happy about that was Casey being there.

God, he needed to wrap his arms around her and forget about all this, just for a little while. It was damn presumptuous of him to assume she'd be willing. They hadn't spoken since she'd left, but he needed some hope to cling to, to get him through this.

"Yup. You are. You can fly back and forth once a month just like Jake used to. He did it, so can you."

"I guess." Bonner wished he were as sure.

"The wake's tonight. You know what you're wearing? You need me to press anything for you?"

Mrs. Jones's mention of the wake reminded Bonner that the viewing of the body at the funeral home was tonight. He'd managed to forget about that.

The wake and the funeral should both be a real joy considering how Jocelyn and J.J. felt about him now.

"I haven't given a thought about what to wear." Bonner shook his head. "And you don't have to wait on me because some piece of paper in a lawyer's office says I'm in charge." He scowled at the idea of being responsible for anything more than Justus and Dakota and the four hundred head.

"Don't you worry. I'm not taking care of you because you're the boss now. I'm helping you because you look like you need it. Besides, I already cook and clean for you. What's a little laundry or ironing too?" She shrugged.

She was right. She'd been taking care of him for a long time now. He let out a short sad laugh at that realization. "Then you might as well tell me what I should wear too, because I have no clue."

"Tonight, I think clean jeans, your good boots and a nice

shirt is fine. Tomorrow you're going to have to be in a suit."

Bonner glanced up. "I don't own a suit."

"No, but the old man does. A bunch of nice ones. You're his size."

"I am?"

"Yup. Maybe a little broader in the arms, but I think you'll fit in the jacket just fine. You didn't know you two wore the same size?"

He shook his head. "No."

Apparently there were all sorts of things he didn't know, including he was kin and heir to the Maverick throne.

It had been one hell of a day. Forget that, it had been one hell of a week, and it wasn't done yet.

"I'll go pick one and you can try it on."

Bonner drew in and blew out a slow breath. "Okay."

"Oh, I almost forgot. There's a memo for you. I heard it come through on the fax machine this afternoon."

Bonner laughed. It was surreal. His life. Jake's will. This new influx of memos. "All right."

She handed him a folded piece of paper. He opened it and saw the corporate letterhead.

"It's not for me. It says it's for the Maverick family, from Jake's assistant, Dean."

Mrs. Jones's brows rose sharply. "And? What are you?"

"Jake's family." Bonner sighed, and then skimmed the text. What he read had him feeling his new responsibilities even more keenly.

He glanced up at Mrs. Jones. "Did you read it?"

She let out a snort. "Of course, I did. It's my job to know what's happening around here."

"The New York office has already received a hundred thousand messages of condolence. Letters. Emails. And he says he can't even begin to keep up with the number of posts on the social media sites Casey set up." Bonner felt the weight of every one of those messages bearing down on him, making it hard to breathe. "A hundred thousand. How can I live up to that? To the man he was?"

Bonner had only known he was a Maverick in blood, if not in name, for such a short time. He still wasn't sure what to do with that news. It wasn't public knowledge yet, but if J.J. and Jocelyn changed their minds and brought this to court, his birthright would come out publicly.

Hell, even if they didn't contest the will, they might decide to be spiteful and bring it to the press. Even a sixty-year-old scandal could take down a company based on family values.

"You can do this, Bonner. I have faith in you. The old man did too."

"How can I do this?" He looked to her for help she couldn't possibly give.

"Well, things have been going pretty good for the past hundred years. Maybe you should look to the past. Let it guide you for the future." Mrs. Jones delivered that advice as if it was the answer to all his problems.

"Look to the past. That's real philosophical." Bonner shook his head. "And then?"

"You'll figure it out. I'll go get you that suit."

Bonner sat alone after she left, not sure he had the energy to move. He remembered the note in his pocket and took it out.

Sliding his callused finger beneath the flap, he tore open the envelope and pulled out a card.

"Bonner. I know what a loss Jake's death is to you. You're in my thoughts. Call if you need anything at all. Casey."

She included her number written beneath her name. It was all Bonner could do to stop himself from dialing it. The only thing that did stop him was the certainty that hearing her voice and having her try to comfort him after the day he'd had would break him for sure.

He rose from the bench and prepared himself to try on Jake's suit. It seemed he'd be not only stepping into the old man's shoes at the company, he'd be filling his suit as well.

~ * ~

After getting over the surreal shock of looking at his reflection in the mirror while he wore Jake's suit, he somehow made it through the rest of the evening.

There was the dinner Mrs. Jones forced upon him even though he had no appetite. That was followed by the wake and the killer looks from his newfound family members. Then questions from Justus and Dakota when he arrived back at the bunkhouse.

He felt bad doing it but he kept the truth about his Maverick connection from them, for the time being anyway.

Finally, Bonner crashed and somehow, thankfully, he slept.

The next thing he was aware of was the bright light of morning creeping in through the window. He never slept past sunrise, yet one look at the clock in his room told him it was well past, and that he'd missed breakfast.

Groaning, he swung his feet to the floor. Today was not the day to oversleep. Besides his regular chores, there was Jake's funeral to deal with, not to mention his very unhappy Maverick relatives.

He threw on some work clothes and headed outside, where he encountered Justus and Dakota with a tail-wagging Misty tagging behind them.

Justus clamped his hat lower onto his head as a gust of wind threatened to take it. "Blue. We got a storm moving in. It's predicted to hit tomorrow."

Dakota folded his gloved hands beneath his arms against the cold. "It's supposed to dump two feet of snow on us over a twenty-four hour period."

"Shit. Why didn't you wake me earlier?" The to-do list grew in Bonner's head.

They'd have to move the herd and get prepared for the storm. That much snow was not only a bitch to deal with, it was dangerous. It could be deadly for both man and beast.

Usually Bonner could sense a big storm moving in even before the weatherman announced it. That he hadn't felt this one was proof of how preoccupied he'd been.

Dakota shrugged. "We thought you needed the rest after all the shit going on."

Bonner shook his head. "Well, next time don't think."

Now was not the time to rest. He had to handle both his own duties, plus Jake's. He'd have to consider hiring on another hand. If Bonner was going to replace Jake, then he'd have to hire someone to replace himself. One thing was sure, the trip to New York would have to wait until the storm passed. Maybe his priorities were messed up, but the herd and the ranch came first.

"All right, Blue." Justus nodded, looking suitably reprimanded by the tone that came out sharper than Bonner meant it to.

"Mrs. Jones put a plate aside for you since you missed breakfast." Dakota supplied that information like a peace offering.

"Thanks." Bonner nodded and turned toward the house.

Maybe some hot coffee and breakfast would make him feel a little less ornery. At least he'd feel less like he was sleepwalking in a waking nightmare.

CHAPTER SIXTEEN

It was a good thing Casey was sitting down when she read the email, because otherwise, she'd have fallen over.

The old man had named Bonner his successor, and he'd be coming to the New York offices to begin assuming his responsibilities.

It didn't make sense. Bonner in New York seemed about as farfetched to her as Bonner on the moon. Then again, Jake Maverick was cowboy to the bone too, just like Bonner, and he'd transitioned very well from ranch to city, every month when he flew in for meetings. In the interim, his assistant here at headquarters kept him up to date on what was happening.

Dean, Jake's assistant—actually, now he'd be Bonner's assistant—was probably her best bet for finding out more about this crazy turn of events.

Casey'd had some interaction with Dean, but it had always been through email. Today, Casey decided to pay the man a visit. She'd be better able to feel him and the situation out in person.

She found him in his office, in a state of organized chaos.

The sheer number of cardboard boxes filled with cards

and letters had her pausing in the doorway. "Um, hi."

A guy probably not long out of college glanced up, a harrowed expression on his face. "Can I help you?"

"I hope so." She pasted on a friendly smile to charm him and dared to enter the room. She tiptoed her high heels around a few boxes and stopped near his desk. "I was wondering if you could tell me Mr. Boyd's schedule. When is he scheduled to be here in the offices? I'm Casey Harrington, by the way. I spent a week at the ranch working with him in October."

Casey extended her hand. He raised his own off the computer's mouse only long enough to shake hers. For a brief moment, Casey feared he wouldn't give her any information, but the guy looked so overwhelmed at the moment, he didn't blink an eye at her question.

"Ms. Harrington. Of course. I booked your travel for that trip." He glanced down at a sticky note on his keyboard. "Mr. Boyd is flying in December sixteenth and will be in New York until the twenty-third. I'll sure be happy to have him here. Maybe he can tell me what to do with all these sympathy cards." Dean glanced down at the clutter encroaching on his personal space.

That explained what was in all the boxes that threatened to consume Dean's office, but what stuck out most for Casey were the dates he'd mentioned. December sixteenth was next week. Bonner would be there the very next week.

So soon.

Casey swallowed hard at the thought of seeing him again. "Wow, just before Christmas. The airports are going to be crazy this time of year."

Not Yampa Valley Regional. But certainly the New York airports, not to mention the city itself, would be packed with holiday travelers.

Talk about trial by fire. Bonner's first exposure to New York was going to be quite an experience.

"Probably but it's the soonest he could get away from the ranch and he wanted to get here before the holidays rather than wait until January. Damn, I still haven't booked the car service to pick him up at the airport." He picked up his phone and started flipping through the holder packed to bursting with business cards. As Casey continued to hover near the desk, Dean glanced up. "I'm sorry, Ms. Harrington. Was there anything else I can help you with?"

"No, thank you, but maybe I can help you."

Casey didn't want Bonner's first sight in New York to be a stranger from the car service holding a sign with his name scribbled on it.

She smiled and prepared to charm Dean into letting her pick up Bonner at the airport. Her heart raced at the thought. She only hoped he'd be as happy to see her again as she would be to see him.

~ * ~

At the airport, Casey began to tremble as she first caught sight of the cowboy hat. It seemed to float above the crowd pouring down the hallway leading away from the gate of the flight arriving from Denver International.

From her position outside of the security checkpoint, she couldn't see a face yet, but it had to be Bonner. She just knew it.

The stream of people scattered and dispersed, and then there he was, looking just as she remembered him, but at the same time, totally different.

She had a moment to take him in before he spotted her—his hat and cowboy boots looked comfortingly familiar, but the dark suit he wore threw her off.

Bonner in a suit was a strange though certainly not a bad sight. He looked good. Very good.

Of course his face was just as she remembered, except that his expression was more somber, maybe a bit concerned. A frown creased his brow as he gazed up at the signs pointing the direction to the baggage claim and ground transportation.

When his familiar blue eyes opened wide as they focused on her standing near the escalator, Casey knew he'd seen her. She smiled and when he smiled back she knew she'd made the right decision to collect him herself.

His long strides ate up the short distance between them, and then he was there in front of her.

She smiled wider. "Hi. Welcome to New York."

"Casey." He pulled her into his arms and though she'd kind of been hoping for a kiss, what she received instead was a hug tight enough to force the air from her lungs.

He held her, unmoving, for a very long time. She felt him breathing hard. If she wasn't mistaken, he was shaking.

Concerned, Casey pulled back from where he'd pressed her face into his chest, just far enough he'd be able to hear. "Hey. You all right?"

He shook his head and didn't ease up on his grip. "No."

Bonner was taking Jake's death far worse than she'd predicted. Casey had known it would be hard on him. They'd been so close for so long, but she'd never thought to find him like this. So...broken.

Not sure what else she could do besides simply be there for him, she squeezed him tighter. "I'm sorry."

"I know. Thanks." He finally pulled back. "Is there someplace we can go?"

"Well, I thought after we get your luggage, we'd get you checked into the hotel. It's the same place Jake always used to stay." His brows knit together and Casey realized Bonner didn't need a cold hotel room right now. He needed the comfort of a home. She continued, "Or I can take you to my place. It's nothing special but it's warm and cozy and is conveniently located near some excellent take-out restaurants, all of which I have on speed-dial."

He looked relieved. "Your place sounds real good."

"Great." Casey put on her cheery face and took his hand in hers. "Come on. Let's grab your bag and get out of here."

On the way down the escalator, Bonner laced his fingers through hers. Casey's heart skipped a beat and she realized it was going to be really hard for her to ever let go of him again.

He held on to her right up until he had to release her hand to pull his suitcase off the luggage carousel, then he grabbed hold of her again.

Casey wasn't about to complain about any kind of physical contact with Bonner. She'd missed the feel of his hands too much since they'd parted, but his demeanor concerned her.

He'd been so in control at the ranch, but here, now, he seemed so uncertain.

She'd have to bolster his confidence and get him ready for the meetings he'd be expected to attend at headquarters. Corporate executives could smell blood in the water. They'd pounce on Bonner and eat him alive if he didn't go in looking strong and in charge.

Casey tried very briefly to make small talk on the drive from the airport to her apartment, but quickly gave up. Not that Bonner had ever been a huge talker, but it was more than obvious he wasn't in the mood for chatter right now.

He stared out the window as the city sped past. She could only imagine what he was thinking as he gazed silently at the ugly buildings and overpasses that blended together in one indiscernible mass of grey.

It was worlds away from his home and he was probably really feeling that about now.

"And we're here." She smiled and pulled into her spot in the parking garage, which cost her as much each month as some people paid in rent. She chose not to tell Bonner that and put the car in park.

The covered lot was dark and dreary and wasn't such a great welcome for Bonner. She hustled to get him and his bag out of there, across the street and up to her apartment where he'd feel better, she was sure.

How could he not with her ever increasing Maverick Western purchases everywhere?

She led the way up the exterior stairs to the door of the building, then unlocked and held it, waiting for him. "Sorry there's no elevator."

"It's okay." He hefted his suitcase up the last few stairs like it weighed next to nothing.

"Most days it's not a problem, but moving day was real

hell." Casey laughed and tried to lighten the mood. Bonner only nodded and stepped inside. She let the front door slam shut behind them. "So one more flight then we're there."

"Okay."

Casey drew in a deep breath and led the way up to her apartment. She unlocked the door and reached in to flip on the lights. She wanted a bright happy space to greet Bonner.

He entered and the surreal look of him, all big and western looking in her tiny city apartment, was hard to absorb.

"This is it. Home sweet home." She closed the door and flipped the deadbolt, then moved to a small table lamp and switched it on. When she turned back, it was to see Bonner setting his suitcase down on the floor. "Are you hungry?"

"No." With a determined look he took off his hat.

He laid it on the table and strode to Casey. Then his lips were pressed against hers. He was hard and demanding. She didn't mind one bit. She melted into his embrace, gladly taking his tongue into her mouth when he pressed it between her lips.

He engulfed her face with his hands, bracing her for the deep kiss. Then he slid them down her body, as if relearning her curves. When he reached the cheeks of her ass, he hoisted her up off her feet. She wrapped her legs around his waist as he groaned against her mouth.

He pulled away just enough to say, "I need you."

His words twisted her heart. "The bedroom's right behind you."

Bonner groaned again and spun them toward the bedroom door. Inside, he dropped her onto the mattress and followed her down, laying his long, hard body over hers. Here, in the bedroom at least, he was the man she remembered.

In charge. In control. Indestructible.

"I've missed you." He breathed the words just shy of her mouth before grabbing a handful of her hair, pulling her head back and crashing his lips into hers again.

Casey ran her hands over his suit jacket, down the planes of his broad, muscular back, to his narrow waist, finally settling on his ass. She spread her legs and pulled him tighter against her.

They were still both fully clothed, but she couldn't resist the delicious friction the outline of the erection inside his pants caused when it rubbed her.

Feeling needy, she moved against him, increasing the pressure.

He rocked his pelvis into her, while stroking his tongue against hers. She'd been so desperate for his touch for so long.

Torn between wanting to get right down to business and wanting this to go slow and last forever, Casey wasn't quite sure what to do. Tear off his suit, lovely though it was, or kiss him until both their lips were sore?

She decided to let Bonner set the pace. He'd been through a lot. She was more than willing to give him whatever he needed right now to heal. To feel whole again.

Bonner seemed different. She sensed his need, the urgency to possess her just like at the cabin, but Casey could also sense a deep shift in him.

This change in his life—Jake's death, his stepping up to the presidency—it weighed upon him. She felt it as much as his weight upon her now, pressing her into the mattress.

She pulled away from his mouth. "Let me get you undressed. Okay?"

Complying easily enough, he nodded and rolled off her. Bonner watched her movements, and helped by moving an arm here, lifting his hips there. But upon closer look, he appeared more like a predator waiting to pounce, than a man allowing her to tend to him.

Undressing him gave her a moment to fully take in the changes in his appearance. His footwear of choice was still cowboy boots, but they were black and looked as if they'd recently been buffed to a high sheen.

His suit was simple but quality. As good as any she'd seen on the male executives at work. Casey was grateful for that. He'd come in to the meetings at HQ on equal footing in the fashion department at least.

The jacket fit his arms a bit too tightly. She supposed he had biceps and forearms larger than the average executive since he pushed cattle not pencils for a living.

She'd have to hook him up with either a custom suit or a retailer who specialized in big and tall. He'd be more comfortable in a jacket that fit properly.

The closely cropped beard that had covered his cheeks and chin while they were at the ranch was gone. He was completely clean-shaven now. She'd kind of enjoyed the rugged look of him unshaven, though kissing him now was definitely easier on the skin of her own face.

Rather than a necktie, he wore a bolo. She smiled as she pulled the braided leather cord and its ornate western style decoration over his head so she could unbutton his shirt.

Even dressed as a businessman, he was still all cowboy. Right down to his shirt. It was a thinner cotton dress shirt than the heavier work shirts he always wore, but it was still the blue she'd come to know and love on him.

She'd like to imagine he'd chosen it just for her.

Once she'd pulled the shirt's sleeves down his arms, he lay temptingly before her in nothing but boxer briefs. Casey ran her hands over the well-developed muscles of his arms, touching his tattoos lightly before sliding to his narrow waist, then lower, pushing the briefs down his strong thighs. His erection sprung up to meet her. She bent and lowered her mouth over it.

Bonner grabbed her arms in a tight grip and hissed in a breath. Opening her eyes, she glanced up to find his eyes squeezed shut and his head pressed deep into the pillow. She moved over him, slow, taking him deep, then pulling back until just the very crown remained in her mouth, before sliding back down again all the way.

The warmth of Bonner's skin made Casey realize she was way overdressed. She didn't want anything between them.

Every inch of him pressed against every inch of her still wouldn't be enough to satisfy the longing, but it would be a good start.

Casey pulled her long-sleeved top over her head and tossed it toward the pile of Bonner's clothes already on the floor. Her shoes and pants followed, until she was only in her bra and panties. The look of lust on Bonner's face clearly showed his appreciation of the view. As did his actions.

He reached out and flipped her onto her back. He hovered over her, his eyes narrowed with desire as he gazed down.

Much like she'd done to him, Bonner skimmed his hands over her body, sliding her panties down her legs. He made short work of her bra, which ended up on the floor with the rest, then he leaned low capturing her breast between his lips, torturing her nipple.

Arching her back, she pressed deeper into the heat of his mouth. He answered the action with a groan while he slid one finger inside her.

Her breast popped from his mouth as he repositioned himself between her legs before giving her what she'd dreamed of since leaving Colorado. As Bonner braced himself above Casey, he plunged his length inside her, forcing a sigh from her lips.

Bonner kept his eyes focused on her face as he stroked in and out. He watched her as she watched him, with a mingled expression of hunger and relief that their joint need was about to be completely satisfied.

Casey's body coiled, poised on the brink of climax as Bonner increased the speed of his stroke. As she lifted her hips off the bed, he slid his hands beneath her and rocked into her faster, hitting every spot she needed him to.

The increase in both of their breathing told of their impending orgasms. Casey grabbed the firm globes of Bonner's ass and pulled him closer as he pounded into her.

That was all it took to push her over the edge. Her muscles clenched around him in orgasmic spasms that had him gasping for breath and finally groaning loud as he plunged and held deep one last time.

He lay on top of her, totally still except for his heavy

breathing, for what seemed like a long time.

Not that she was complaining. Bonner's weight upon her, his length, still firm though fading inside her, was what she'd longed for during every lonely night she'd spent in this bed since meeting him.

"I really missed doing this with you." She kissed his chest and stroked his back.

"Me too." Bonner let out a short laugh that vibrated through her. Finally he pushed himself up. "We need to talk about some stuff."

His stomach let out a loud rumble, causing Casey to frown. "I think we need to order dinner too. When was the last time you ate something?"

"Mrs. Jones made me something before I left for the airport this morning."

"Then you're long overdue. I'll order, then we'll talk and eat. Deal?"

"And uh, maybe some more of what we just did?" The old Bonner she knew and loved was starting to resurface.

"Oh, definitely. And if I remember correctly our discussion in the cabin, the next time should be your favorite position." Casey smiled.

"I'm finding with you, every position is my favorite." He cupped her face in his hands and kissed her.

She broke away and groaned.

"Keep this up and we're never getting out of this bed." Actually, they really didn't have to. She held up one finger. "Hang on for just one minute. I can fix this. What Chinese food do you like to eat?"

"Got me." Bonner shrugged and was paying much more attention to running the tip of his finger around the darkened edge of her nipple than to her question.

"I'll just get us an assortment." Casey swatted his hand away and reached for the cell phone in the pocket of her pants on the floor. She found the number for China Gourmet in her contact list and dialed. "Hi, I'd like to order take out for delivery... Casey Harrington... Yes, you have me in the database... Yup, that's me... Um, one order of Pepper Steak. One General Tao's Chicken. Two egg rolls. A large Pork Fried Rice. Oh, and one order fried dumplings. You have my credit card on file? ...Great. How long?... Thanks."

Bonner's brows rose. "You really don't cook, do you?"

"Nope." She rolled toward him, biting her lip. "That make you think less of me?"

His gaze dropped to where he skimmed his hand over the curve of her hip. "Nope. How much time we got 'til the food's here?"

"They said twenty minutes or so." She smiled at the look of hunger in his eyes. It wasn't only food he wanted. "Why?"

"I have an idea how to kill the time." His body showed he was more than ready again. "Roll over."

Casey pursed her lips but did as he asked. "I thought you wanted to talk."

"Later." Lifting her ass high in the air, he was inside her before she could respond.

His having come moments before did nothing to diminish Bonner's performance.

He finished in the time allowed, though Casey wouldn't have minded if they could have gotten an extension.

She'd just gotten herself cleaned up in the bathroom and was pulling her Maverick lounging pants on under the shirt she'd taken from Bonner in Colorado when the doorbell rang.

Her path to the door took her past the kitchen table where Bonner's hat lay. Just the sight of it made her smile.

She took the large bag from the deliveryman, signed the credit card receipt and added a tip.

Skirting Bonner's suitcase on the floor, she left the food on the kitchen counter and turned toward the bedroom.

As Casey padded back to Bonner, stretched out naked and gorgeous on her bed, she realized two things—she could get very used to this and to do so would be very dangerous.

CHAPTER SEVENTEEN

Dressed in nothing but his long dress shirt and boxer briefs, Bonner let out a big breath, his belly full to bursting. He leaned against the chair back. "That was a lot of food."

Casey laughed and looked over the remains on the table. "You did it justice."

"Yeah, guess I was hungrier than I thought." Bonner glanced at her sweet face, framed by the collar of the shirt she'd taken from him back at the cabin. Just the sight of her warmed him. He only wished he could be touching her too, but she was on the other side of the table. "Can we put this stuff away later and just sit together for a bit?"

"Sure. We can snuggle on the couch under my Maverick Western Buffalo Plaid Throw. It's perfect to give as a gift or to keep for yourself."

"So I've heard." He laughed. "Sounds perfect."

She took his hand, while eyeing him closely, as if she knew he needed to hold her while they talked.

They made their way to the sofa, and sure enough, there was the plaid throw. She arranged it over their laps. He put his arm around her and pulled her closer, needing her strength as his own flagged.

New York was so foreign to him. The corporate offices where he was expected to lead an entire company would be even more so.

"You're going to do great, you know."

He glanced down at her as she looked up at him. "How can you know that?"

"Well first off, I'm very good at my job and I'll be behind you all the way. Second, I did some looking into your assistant Dean. He's young but he's way overqualified for the position. He can handle much more than just booking flights and meetings, or sorting through your mail. I think giving him more responsibility will keep him from eventually getting bored and moving on to another company. He can be a real right hand man for you here, so use him."

"All right." Bonner absorbed all she was saying. It made sense but didn't exactly belay his fear of standing in front of all the corporate executives and being laughed out of the office for being an uneducated cowboy, just like J.J. had said.

He let out a sigh, and Casey responded by slipping an arm around him and squeezing. "Let me tell you something. You can take a fish out of the water, but that doesn't make him a less valuable fish."

Bonner genuinely laughed at that, long and hard. "So you're saying I'm the fish in this situation. Uh, thanks, I guess?"

"You're no more the fish than I was. Look, I was marketing a German-based bank this time last year. Now, I'm helping sell the Western lifestyle and philosophy. Since I joined the company and started the new social marketing campaign, sales have increased fifteen percent over the same period last year."

"Congratulations. That's something to be proud of."

"Thanks, but I'm not looking for compliments. What I'm saying is this—actually this is a good idea and I think we should plan it after the New Year—but anyway, if you were to fly all the corporate big wigs from Maverick Western out to the ranch in Colorado, throw them into a saddle and smack the horse's ass, they would be just as insecure and out of place as you feel in the offices here."

"But the difference is, they haven't been put in charge of the ranch. I have been put in charge of the company."

God help them all.

Casey shook her head. "What you're not getting is that you don't have to be an expert at all of their jobs. The CFO and his accounting department don't expect or need you to be a CPA. Just like I don't need you to know how to market Maverick Western. We're good at our jobs. That's why we have them. What we need you for is to remind us why we're there. To help us and the customer remember the philosophy and the example that John Maverick set a hundred years ago. I can't think of a man more perfect to take Jake's place in that."

Wow, she really was good at her job. She even had him believing he could do it. "That's what Jake said too."

She frowned. "Did you know he was leaving control of the company to you before he died?"

Bonner shook his head and let out a short laugh. "No, not even close. But that brings us to what I wanted to talk to you about."

Casey nodded slowly. "Okay."

Bonner drew in a deep breath. She needed to know all of it. There was no doubt in Bonner's mind Casey would keep his confidence about his birthright, but it was important she be prepared with the truth. If Jocelyn and J.J. decided to go public with this information sometime down the road, it would be Casey and her department doing damage control and trying to save the company's reputation.

He swallowed away the dryness in his mouth and launched into the tale that he was still having trouble believing himself.

CHAPTER EIGHTEEN

His hands were sweating. His armpits too. Thank God the suit jacket would hide that, even though it felt more like a straight-jacket at the moment.

Bonner ran his finger between the collar of his shirt and his throat.

In the privacy of Jake's, now Bonner's office, Casey pressed her palms to his face and stared directly into his eyes. "Listen to me. You're going to be great and they're all going to love you. Trust me."

He braced his hands on her waist, wishing they could give up on all this and just go back to her place. "I do trust you."

"Good." She nodded, looking full of the confidence he wished he felt as strongly as she did. "You ready?"

He swallowed hard. "Yes."

She led the way toward the boardroom. It was all he could do to not reach for her hand for comfort, because waiting inside was everyone of any importance in this company. Jake's company. Now, his company.

Dean, who was as young as Casey had described but hopefully also as capable, stood outside the closed door of the room. "They're all inside, Mr. Boyd. Another copy of the seating chart listing their names and positions is in the folder at your seat, in case you need it."

"Thank you." He'd spent an hour trying to memorize it last night at Casey's place, right after she'd shown him how to get into his new corporate email account from her computer and download a PDF file, whatever the hell that stood for.

Heart pounding, Bonner drew in a breath and nodded to Dean.

He had a strange feeling of transcending time, as if he was on the back of a bull in the chute nodding to the gateman, the adrenaline surging through his veins making him feel superhuman. He embraced the long forgotten feeling.

As the door swung wide, Bonner stepped aside and motioned for Casey to go in first. Her lips twitched with a smile. She walked to the head of the long table inside the room.

He strode in after her with more confidence than he'd known he could muster.

She faced the assembled executives. "Ladies. Gentlemen. It's with pleasure I introduce to you the new president of Maverick Western. He was Jake Maverick's right arm for ten years at the family ranch and it's only fitting he step up to fill his shoes at Maverick Western. I give you Bonner Boyd."

Casey stepped to the side and to his amazement the group began to applaud.

Hell, they more than clapped, they got to their feet. His gaze swept the men and women standing for him.

Bonner swallowed away the lump in his throat and waited for the applause to start to die down. "Thank you. Please, take your seats."

He waited as they did, hoping he remembered what he wanted to say. The words he'd been up most of the night working out in his head.

The other half of the night he'd been awake burying his fears and frustration inside Casey. He shot a glance at her, then looked back at the faces of each and every person seated at the table.

"Jake Maverick told me something years ago, but it always stuck with me. He said, 'Bonner, you'll find there are two kinds of men in this world. There are doers, and there are talkers, and the interesting thing is, a man is never both because the doers are too busy doing to be talking, and the talkers are too busy talking to be doing.'"

He glanced down the table and noticed smiles and nods, and a particularly proud look on Casey's face.

He cleared his throat and went on. "You'll find I'm not a man who has a lot to say, but I guess that's a good thing according to the old man...uh, I mean Jake—"

There were chuckles throughout the audience. Bonner smiled at his own slip. "I never called him that to his face, mind you, but I don't think he would have minded. He always called things the way he saw them, just like I do. Anyway, I'm a good listener. I appreciate a good day's work. I'm not the most educated man you'll ever meet, but I'm smart enough to know a person never stops learning, even if he lives to be a hundred. And lastly, if you need anything from me, just ask. Whether I'm here in New York or in Colorado, Dean will know how to get in touch with me. Otherwise, quite honestly, as long as you all keep up the values and the mission Maverick Western has represented for the past hundred years, I'm smart enough to know to stay out of your way and let you do your jobs. You all know what you're doing or Jake wouldn't have put you where you are. So, that's it. That's all I've got to say."

The applause resumed, louder than before.

He glanced at Casey for help. She stepped forward and the room got silent.

"Does anyone have any questions?" When no one stepped up to ask him anything, she nodded. "All right. Then I guess we're done here. Dean has scheduled meetings between Mr. Boyd and each department head over the next week so you'll all get to speak with him one on one and familiarize Mr. Boyd with your particular department. Thank you."

There were lots of hands to shake, as Bonner tried to

connect names to faces, then the room cleared except for him, Dean and Casey.

She smiled. "You did really well."

"Thanks. They were really…receptive."

"Of course they were. I've been building up to this for the past week. Press releases. Daily blog posts. All about you. I wanted everyone to know you and appreciate what a good choice Jake made before they met you."

"Wow. Thanks." Bonner itched to touch her, but Dean being there stopped him. He glanced at his assistant. "So, what next?"

Dean whipped a piece of paper out of his folder. "I've printed out your schedule for today, then I have the rest of the week mapped out, both daily and a weekly overview. It's all printed out in here. You know, I could order you a tablet. Then you can see any updates in the schedule in real time."

Dean held up a device that matched the one tucked under Casey's arm and Bonner laughed. "Can we stick to paper for now?"

"Sure. Anyway, you'll see your next meeting isn't for an hour, so you have a break." Dean pointed to the paper.

"Good. Thank you. I, uh, think I'd like to go over some marketing things with Miss Harrington as long as I have the time. If she's available?" Bonner shot Casey a hope-filled look.

"I have some time." She smiled.

"Okay." Dean nodded. "I'll come to your office in time to show you to your next meeting."

"Thanks, Dean." Bonner barely noticed the man leave. He only had eyes for Casey. The moment the door closed behind his assistant, Bonner stepped forward and pulled Casey into his arms. "Thank you."

"For what?"

"For everything." He pressed her close and then laughed. "Is it horrible the only thing I can think about is bending you over that table and loving you until we both can't stand?"

Casey laughed. "Funny. I was just thinking about the same

thing." She glanced behind her. "We could lock the door."

Damn, now he had a hard-on. "Stop tempting me. I can't do something like that my first day."

"That's fine. I can wait until your second day." She looked devilish.

"Thanks. I appreciate that." He laughed. "How about a compromise. I'm willing to go back to my office and maybe make out for a little while."

She grinned. "Sounds good."

He felt lighter. As if the weight of a world of worry was slowly lifting off his shoulders.

Could it be possible this whole thing was really going to work out? That he actually could pull off being president?

Bonner was afraid to even think it.

CHAPTER NINETEEN

Bonner moved above Casey, slow, easy, in the early morning light of her bedroom. He dipped lower and kissed her mouth.

She felt the new grown stubble on his face that made him look so rugged. Unlike at the ranch, he shaved everyday here. She missed seeing the shadow on his chin. She missed his cute ass encased in jeans too, since he'd worn a suit every day.

But she sure hadn't had to miss his sexy as hell body. They'd been like teenagers the past week, having sex in every room of her apartment, both day and night. Though he hadn't given in to her teasing and done it in the office…Yet.

After having him in her bed every night over the past week, the thought of being alone tomorrow night brought a tear to her eye. She brushed it away and he stilled.

"What's wrong?"

"Nothing."

"Casey. Tell me."

"You want to talk now?" She forced a laugh, and glanced down to where they were joined.

"Yes. You're crying while I'm making love to you. Something's wrong."

"There's nothing you can do about it so just ignore me and keep going. Okay?" She swiped at another tear as it escaped and ran down the side of her face.

"No. I'm not going to keep going while you're crying."

"You have to because this time tomorrow you'll be at the airport. It's now or never." Her voice cracked on the last word.

"It's because I'm leaving." He sighed and pulled out. He rolled to lie next to her. "I don't know what to say, Casey. I have to get back to the ranch. Tell me how to fix this."

"There's nothing to fix. You live in Colorado. I live here. I'll see you when you're here for your meetings or when I'm there for my work. If you want to see me, that is."

"Of course I want to. I wouldn't be here if I didn't. Is that what you want? To...do this when we can?"

"Yes." She said yes even though she meant no.

Casey hated the idea of only being with Bonner a few days a month. She hated the thought of saying goodbye to him, over and over again. If they continued like this, she'd be saying it a lot. And what if he met someone there in Colorado and got serious with her?

He reached out and brushed a hand over her cheek as another tear trailed down. "Then why are you crying?"

Good question. Casey Harrington didn't cry over men. Hell, she didn't cry about anything...well, except that final scene in that one Christmas movie.

"I don't know. PMS?" Getting her emotions in check, she grabbed his hand and kissed the palm, then rolled over on top of him. As she slid him inside her, she leaned low. "I bet you can cheer me up though."

His eyelids drifted partially closed. "I'll surely try."

He flipped them over and loved her, long and slow until they both forgot her tears as first Casey, then Bonner reached completion.

Still shaking and breathless, with Bonner's weight heavy on top of her, Casey decided she could do this. They could do this. They would have to.

They'd enjoy each other when they were in the same state, then concentrate on their respective jobs while they were apart.

It really was perfect. She was focused on her career right now anyway. She couldn't have designed a better arrangement.

So why did her heart hurt so badly at the thought of him leaving tomorrow?

CHAPTER TWENTY

The line moved. Jody and Casey, with Jenna and Courtney ahead of them, took one step forward. They stopped and Casey sighed. "We could come back later."

"Patience, Aunt Casey." Jody sent her a smile. "We're almost there."

Attempting to see the holiday windows at Saks Fifth Avenue on the day before Christmas Eve had not been a good idea. There had to be a hundred people lined up within the maze of ropes and stanchions set up on the sidewalk in front of the store to keep them orderly.

This might be fun for tourists, out-of-towners like her sister, but for Casey, who walked these streets daily, it was simply annoying.

"Fine." She sighed. "But we better keep our eye on the time so we don't miss our reservation."

High tea at The Plaza and then a shopping trip to FAO Schwartz had been a holiday tradition for Casey and her sister since her nieces had been infants in a stroller.

"We won't miss it." Jody sent her a sideways glance. "Why didn't he just stay for Christmas and then fly back?"

The question would have seemed totally out of the blue if

Casey didn't know for a fact she was acting like a miserable bitch today, and the reason was because she'd dropped Bonner at the airport this morning before meeting her sister at Grand Central.

Her chest felt so tight, it hurt to even breathe deeply. "He can't be away from the ranch for too long. And he knew I had plans with you for Christmas."

Besides, Casey knew he considered Mrs. Jones, Dakota and Justus family too. Of course he'd want to be home with them for the holiday.

"You know very well you could have brought him to any family event, including our girls' day out today. You know at least one of them would have freaked out to meet a real cowboy in person." Jody glanced at her daughters.

The girls were occupied with counting the number of people in front of them so Casey could speak freely. "Yes, I know. But no way in hell was I going to subject Bonner to Mom. And it's not like we're dating. We're just..."

There was no way to hide it. Casey had canceled Bonner's reservation at the hotel the first night knowing he'd be in her bed every night and he had been.

"Yeah, I know." Jody raised a brow. "What I don't understand is why?"

Casey laughed. "Why? Have you seen him?"

Jody rolled her eyes. "That's not what I meant and you know it. I meant why aren't you two more? Why can't you have a relationship? You're obviously compatible. He seems more than interested in you. You're practically glowing when you talk about him. So why not?"

"Um, hello? Do you realize how many miles there are between Colorado and New York?"

More than just miles separated them. Bonner and Casey lived in different worlds. City and country.

Though Bonner had made the transition to the corporate world beautifully this week, she knew a part of him would die should he ever move to the city permanently. And he was in charge of the ranch too. He needed to divide his time.

Casey glanced between the buildings and spotted the huge evergreen set up at Rockefeller Center. Its colored lights and the star on top twinkled in the grey December light.

She loved this city, especially at Christmas time. The line advanced another foot. The pushy group of people behind them bumped into Casey and she realized there were things she didn't love about it too, especially at Christmas time.

"Plenty of couples make a long distance relationship work. Some are even bi-coastal. At least Colorado is only half-way across the country." Jody continued talking. "I don't know. I just think you should at least talk about it. And you should have planned to spend Christmas together. You still could."

"He's already in the air by now."

"So? Join him. I can't think of a more beautiful place to spend the holiday than on a snowy ranch in the Colorado mountains. You should just go."

Casey frowned at her sister. "Are you crazy? It's the day before Christmas Eve."

"Exactly. You can be there by Christmas. Get yourself to the airport and on a stand-by list."

She shook her head. "Every flight is going to be packed."

Jody waved her hand dismissively at that. "You can't tell me every single seat on every flight to Colorado will be booked. You're one person. They'll slip you in. Now, when Kent, the girls and I fly to the ranch to visit you for the holidays next year, of course I'll make reservations well in advance. I wouldn't expect them to accommodate a family of four on a last minute flight." Jody smiled.

The scene she'd set of what Casey's life could be like this time next year had her heart fluttering. She hadn't known it until now, but she wanted that. A real home. A family. Bonner. Even kids of their own.

"What if he doesn't want the same thing? What if he's happy with what we have? You know, just—" Casey glanced to see where the girls were before whispering "—casual sex."

Jody let out a laugh. "From what you've told me, this man is anything but casual. Just go. What will it hurt to spend the holidays together and see how things feel? I'm not saying you should give up the lease on your apartment and change your driver's license to Colorado. Just go and see."

A sense of urgency pressed like a physical weight upon Casey. "I should get to the airport as soon as possible if I want to have any hope of getting there by Christmas."

"Then go."

She paused. "You and the girls—"

"—will be just fine. I may not be the city girl you are, but I can get us to the Plaza and then back to Grand Central." Jody pulled Casey into a hug. "Say good-bye to them and then get the hell out of here. Go get your cowboy for Christmas. You've been waiting a long time for him."

Teary-eyed, Casey laughed. "Yeah. I have."

Funny how things worked out. Twenty-years after her only wish for Christmas had been the Cowboy Cody doll, Casey was finally going to get what she wanted. But even more because unlike Cody, Bonner was very real.

Casey somehow managed to hail one of the few available taxicabs—years of being a New Yorker gave her an advantage over the tourists in that area. Though the holiday gridlock had traffic moving so slowly, she probably could have walked faster.

By the time she was back on her block, she was agitated and keenly feeling the time crunch. She had to throw a few things in a bag and get to the airport.

She was feeling so rushed, it wasn't until she paid the cab and had started up the stairs outside her building that she saw Bonner sitting on the top step. His coat was buttoned up and pulled close to this throat, his hat tipped low over his face. It was a strange and wonderful sight.

"Bonner?" She sprinted up the remainder of the steps. He was here, but for how long?

"Hey." He stood. "I couldn't leave."

"Why not? Was your flight canceled?" She reached out and grabbed his hands, cold from waiting outside for her.

"No." He kissed her and she nearly stopped caring about

the answer to her question. Finally, he pulled back. "I called the ranch and the boys seemed all right without me for a little longer, so I called Dean. I asked him to change my return flight and to send me a car and driver at the airport. I figure if I'm going to be the president of Maverick Western, I could take advantage of the perks every once in a while."

Still shocked, she couldn't help but smile. "I'm really glad you did."

"Me too." He tilted his head toward the door. "Can we go inside?"

"Of course."

He glanced at the sky. "There's a storm coming. There'll be snow before morning."

She could barely breathe but she managed to answer, "That would be nice, but it never snows here in the city for Christmas."

Bonner shrugged. "Feels like snow."

Casey was shaking so badly, with excitement or adrenaline or just from being near Bonner, she could barely get the key in the door.

Finally, she had them inside, upstairs, and in her nice, warm apartment.

Once inside, with the door shut, Bonner peeled off his coat. He tossed it onto a chair and pulled her close. "I couldn't seem to leave you."

"I was coming home to pack a bag and try to get a flight to be with you in Colorado. I couldn't stand the thought of being away from you either. Especially not at Christmas. Or ever." She needed him to know that.

Bonner shook his head. "We make quite a pair, don't we? City girl. Country boy. We can't live together, but we don't want to live apart."

"We'll make it work. You'll be in New York monthly visiting headquarters. I'll fly to you in Colorado whenever I can. At least once a month. Maybe more." She had plenty of frequent flier miles.

"I guess. It's not exactly the ideal situation."

"No, it's not." Casey wanted to fall asleep in his arms each night, and wake to him making love to her each morning, not just a few times a month.

"Casey, I don't know much about this corporate stuff, but I have a question. Why are the corporate offices in New York and the warehousing in New Jersey when the company was founded in Colorado?"

Keeping hold of his hand, she led them to the sofa and took a seat. "Well, I guess when they made the decision it made sense. When Maverick Western began importing products and materials for production, it made sense to put the offices and the warehouses near the shipping facilities in Jersey."

From his seat next to her, Bonner shook his head. "Why are we importing materials? Why aren't we using things from right here in the U.S.?"

"I don't know. That decision was made years ago."

He scowled. "Probably the few years Jake's son, Junior, worked for the company right after college. Before he left and went to a different company."

"No wonder Jake left control to you."

"I guess." He shrugged. "You know, Mrs. Jones said something to me the night of Jake's wake. She said to look to the past to make decisions for the future. Why can't we go back to the way things were originally when John Maverick founded the company? Even if we do have to ship things farther to get them to and from Colorado, it would be Americans we're putting to work doing the trucking. That's a good thing. No?"

"Yes, it is a good thing. But accounting would have to crunch the numbers. Even after the initial cost of the move, it might cost the company all of its profits to have the facilities in Colorado."

Bonner shook his head. "I haven't been here long but I've noticed one thing. Things cost ten times as much here in New York as they do back home."

Casey considered that. "You might be right. The cost of

having production and warehousing in the mid-West might be considerably less. All those years ago when they made the decision to move to Jersey things were probably much cheaper there than they are now. But closing the Maverick facilities wouldn't be a popular move. There'll be backlash from laying off all the East Coast employees if you close them."

"We could make the transition slow and even after it's done, we could still maintain a smaller distribution and shipping center here on the East Coast. Maybe even open it up once a year to the public, as like an outlet center to get rid of overstocks and any old stuff to make room for new products. Folks like that kind of thing, don't they?"

"Yes, they do." She smiled. "You have a better head for this than you give yourself credit for."

"No." He shook his head. "I feel so far out of my world I can't even tell you."

"Kind of like how I felt on a horse, or in the outhouse?"

He let out a short laugh. "Yeah, kind of like that, except you only had me watching, and I was already on your side. I've hundreds of employees and a few million customers worldwide watching me. I'm sure quite a few of them are just waiting for me to fail."

"Nobody's waiting for you to fail." Casey gave his hand a squeeze.

Bonner cocked up a brow. "My dear Maverick cousins are."

"Then it will be extra satisfying to rub it in their faces when you succeed."

Bonner laughed. "Now, now, that attitude's not exactly in keeping with cowboy code is it?"

"No, but it is in keeping with the New York code. You're in my world for now, and even though I might not be so great at riding a horse, I am excellent at swimming with the sharks. I've been preparing for a challenge like this my whole life. If you decide this move is what you want, I can get you and Maverick Western through this transition and we'll come out on top. Trust me."

"I wonder if Jake knew. If that's why he hired you when he did." His face took on an expression of sadness.

"Knew what?"

"That he didn't have much time. His doctor had been warning him his health wasn't good for a while. And the lawyer told me the will naming me had been drawn up in October, right about the time he hired you. It's like he suspected he didn't have long. He'd known that I'd need help." His blue gaze captured hers. "That I'd need you."

Her heart warmed. "Maybe he did know. We won't let him down, Bonner. Trust me on this."

"I do." His sincerity had her eyes misting with tears.

Casey deflected the overwhelming emotions with work. "My head's already spinning with plans for the new marketing campaign. Taking the company back to grass roots. Moving the facilities back to Colorado where it all began. A focus on products made with American materials by American hands. Jake was an imposing character, but you... Bonner with you as the face of the company, every woman will want you and every man will want to be you. And since they can't, they'll do the next best thing—buy Maverick products."

"Now wait a minute." A cocky grin bowed his lips. "Who says all those women can never have me?"

"They'll have to get through me first." Casey narrowed her eyes at the idea.

He stood and pulled her up off the cushion and wrapped his arms around her.

"But you'll be in New York and I'll be in Colorado..." Still grinning, he let the sentence trail off suggestively.

"Or I could be in Colorado. Even if the executive offices remain in New York, with the focus of the corporation moving to Colorado, it makes sense the head of marketing would too."

It was so clear to her now. She loved the city, but she loved Bonner far more. And all the good parts of New York would be here at her disposal whenever she wanted. All she had to do was book a plane ticket.

"You'd do that? Move out west?" There was no more joking. His tone was deadly serious.

"In a heartbeat. If you, as the new corporate president, invited me." She let the suggestion dangle.

"As the new corporate president, I'd never force you to move for your job. But as just me, the guy who can't get you out of his head, who may never sleep again unless you're next to him, I'd like nothing more than for you to move to the ranch and never leave."

Her happiness threatened to bubble over. "Well, I might have to leave sometime, for meetings back here."

"That's fine, because I could come with you."

"Yes. You could."

Traveling together. Enjoying the ranch while she was there with Bonner. Showing him around the city while they were here. It sounded like heaven.

Bonner cradled her face in his palms and stared into her eyes. "I'm so in love with you."

Tears formed in Casey's eyes. "I'm in love with you, too."

He smiled before lowering his mouth to hers. The kiss seemed even sweeter because Bonner loved her.

She had to know something before she could let herself completely enjoy Bonner. "When do you fly back?"

"I had Dean book it for December twenty-seventh. I wanted to be with you for Christmas."

"I'm really glad about that."

Jody had been right. It looked as if Cassie would finally get her cowboy for Christmas.

She glanced out the window and what she saw made her look twice. "Bonner."

"Hm?" He was more occupied with kissing her neck than anything else.

"Look outside." Amazed, she watched as the biggest, fattest flakes of snow she'd ever seen drifted past her window.

He pulled back and glanced at the window. "Told ya it felt

like snow."

A cowboy and a white Christmas.

As Bonner pulled her closer and nuzzled her neck, Casey smiled. She must have been a very good girl this year.

ABOUT THE AUTHOR

A top 10 *New York Times* bestseller, Cat Johnson writes the *USA Today* bestselling Hot SEALs series. Known for her creative marketing, Cat has sponsored bull riding cowboys, promoted romance using bologna and owns a collection of cowboy boots and camouflage for book signings.

Check out more of Cat's contemporary romance, featuring hot alpha heroes who often wear cowboy or combat boots.

Visit CatJohnson.net
Join the mailing list at catjohnson.net/news

Made in the USA
San Bernardino, CA
08 January 2017